THE ITALIAN'S SUMMER SEDUCTION: THE ITALIAN'S PRICE

Diana Hamilton

First published in Great Britain 2006
Large Print edition 2011
Harlequin Mills & Boon Limited,
Eton House, 18-24 Paradise Road, Richmond, Surrey TW9 1SR

© Diana Hamilton 2006

ISBN: 978 0 263 22301 9

Harlequin Mills & Boon policy is to use papers that are natural, renewable and recyclable products and made from wood grown in sustainable forests. The logging and manufacturing process conform to the legal environmental regulations of the country of origin.

Printed in Great Britain
by Clays Ltd, St Ives plc

Hot-blooded, passionate men who have everything—except brides…

MEDITERRANEAN MEN

The all-new Mediterranean Men large-print collection gives you top stories from your favourite glitzy Modern collections in easier-to-read print.

6 addictive large-print volumes

Diana Hamilton started writing for Mills & Boon in 1986, and published over fifty novels. More than twenty million copies of her stories were sold world-wide. Sadly Diana Hamilton died peacefully on 3rd May, 2009, at her home in Shropshire, surrounded by her family. Diana Hamilton will be missed by millions of readers around the globe.

CHAPTER ONE

INSTRUCTING THE TAXI driver to wait, Cesare Saracino swung his long legs to the wet pavement and headed towards the small, old-fashioned butcher's shop at the end of the largely deserted narrow high street, his dark eyes grim with determination.

His investigator had tracked down her widowed mother's home address with no difficulty at all. Personally he couldn't see Jilly Lee actually returning here, never mind living in a flat above a butcher's in a small market town on the border of Wales where nothing much ever happened. She needed bright lights, the company of admiring free-spending males. Glitz and glamour.

She wouldn't be here but her mother would

know where she had gone since her sneaky disappearance from the villa. Jilly Lee—a soft and silly name for a first class bitch— would be made to pay. He'd find her and haul her back to Tuscany, demand reparation, force her to put her hunt for a wealthy husband and her thieving activities on hold and do the job she'd been hired to do.

His mouth tightened with pain. The way things were going, Jilly Lee wouldn't be in harness for long. Nonna was visibly growing more frail, though it galled him to have to admit that since the arrival of the Lee woman she'd brightened considerably.

'There are no signs of clinical disease,' her specialist had informed him three months ago, early in the new year. 'But your grand- mother is well over eighty and has been a widow for how long?'

'Thirty years.'

'And one by one she will have seen most of her contemporaries pass away. The body gets increasingly frail and so the will to live dwindles, there is less and less to look forward to.'

Hating the thought that Nonna was simply letting go, he'd kicked against it and suggested hiring a congenial companion.

'Someone to read to me while I do my embroidery? And drone on in a tedious, elderly way about the misdeeds of modern day youngsters and bore me with interminable tales of her own long-gone youth?' She'd patted his hand, her smile, as ever, kind and fond. 'I don't think so.'

'Someone to keep you company.'

'Rosa can do that.'

'Rosa has her hands full of housekeeping duties. She can't spare the time to go around the garden with you while you snip things off!'

A dry look. 'There are plenty of gardeners to pick me up if I fall over while I'm deadheading—if that's what worries you!'

He'd taken both her frail hands in his. 'I spend as much time here at the villa as I can but I'm often away. Of course I worry about you. You took me in when I was a stroppy twelve-year-old. You cared for me. Let me now care for you. And there's no law that says a paid companion has to be in her dotage.'

He'd drafted the advertisement himself, offered sky-high wages, sat in on the interviews and had noted the first spark of any real interest in the faded old eyes when Jilly Lee had been shown in.

On first sight she'd seemed vaguely familiar. A face glimpsed at a nightclub in Florence when he'd been entertaining an American client who'd expressed an interest in unwinding in a hot spot? But then these out-on-the-prowl bimbos all looked alike. Flowing long blonde hair, pouty scarlet lips, skimpy dresses designed to show pneumatic bosoms and endless legs. Ten a penny. He'd been hit on by enough of them during his thirty-four years to know the type. No wonder Nonna called him cynical.

He'd dismissed the impression. True, Ms Lee had long silky blonde hair but it had been neatly tied back with a black velvet band and the blue shift dress she'd been wearing, although doing nothing to detract from her blatant curves, was demure enough in the hemline stakes.

As in the three previous interviews he'd simply observed, leaving Nonna to run the show, only inputting when he'd felt the need for clarification.

On the face of it she had seemed ideal. Twenty-five years old, so definitely not the middle-aged bore Nonna had stated she wouldn't countenance. English, but with very passable Italian. Excellent references from a famous London store. The time spent in the interim travelling in Italy, picking up the language, taking odd jobs to eke out her savings, moving on, never staying in one place for very long. Now she wanted to settle permanently in this beautiful country.

Rarely sparing him a glance, she'd chatted away with ease, charming and outgoing, and when Nonna—already captivated—had asked her to withdraw for a moment, told him with the first flash of excitement he'd seen coming from her in months, 'I like her. She's young, lively and lovely to look at. Just what I need since you point blank refuse to marry and bring a young bride here to brighten my days and keep me on my toes! Plus, we can practice my English together. I once spoke it as well as you do, but now I am rusty. What do you think? Shall we hire her?'

He hesitated, but only for a moment. She might seem ideal but something about this latest applicant struck a false note. An annoying niggle with nothing concrete to back it up.

With a small impatient shrug he dismissed it. Nonna liked her, which was the main thing. She was showing real enthusiasm for the first time in ages, which meant that she wouldn't just let go, give up the will to live.

'If that's what you want.'

He would do anything for Nonna. He owed her so much. She had been the first person to give him any real affection. His parents hadn't shown any, to him or each other. It had been a dynastic marriage gone wrong. His father, a workaholic, had rarely been home and his mother, to compensate, had spent money like water and taken a string of lovers.

He could only suppose they had stayed married for the sake of appearances. In the circles they moved in appearances were everything.

On their death in a light aircraft accident on one of the rare occasions when they'd been attending the same function together, he had become heir to the vast family-run business enterprise that ranged from the petrochemical industry through luxury hotels to dealing in fine art and precious gems.

Nonna had helped him come to terms with everything. The business was to be run by his late father's hand-picked executive managers until he reached his majority, of course, but she had hired a private tutor to help him learn all he could about his future inheritance, a project he had eagerly embraced.

He could deny her nothing, but caution, and that niggle, had made him add, 'I'll do some rescheduling and stick around for the first few weeks to make sure you suit each other.'

A stab of anger shot through him now as he entered the dank passageway which obviously led to the door to the above-the-shop premises. Jilly Lee had charmed his grandmother into trusting her implicitly, into relying on her company, into actually enjoying what the scheming minx had called 'Girl-talk'. And had done a runner when he'd made it plain that he didn't want her in his bed and wasn't in the market for marriage. Taking a whole load of the old lady's cash with her.

He would make her pay. In spades. He stabbed a finger on the bell-push.

Milly Lee flicked on the overhead light and drew the skimpy curtains over the window to shut out the depressing sight of the wet April evening. It hadn't stopped raining all day. The interior of the small living area was just as chilly and depressing and she wouldn't have stayed here a moment longer than necessary after her mother's death—would just have found herself an inexpensive bedsit with enough room for one—but Jilly wouldn't know how to contact her if she did that and since she'd left her job in Florence Milly had no means of contacting her.

That her identical twin was thoughtless went without saying, but that didn't mean Jilly wouldn't get in touch at some stage, when she finally remembered her family back home. Sadly she reflected that Jilly didn't even know that their mother had passed away. She would be gutted. So, until her twin remembered that she had a family who worried about her and made contact, she would have to stay put.

Pushing the floppy fringe of her short blonde hair out of her eyes, she opened the local evening paper she'd bought on her way home from work and optimistically turned to the Situations Vacant column.

She was going to need to find a new job.

Manda, her boss, had told her this morning that she was selling up. She and her husband wanted to start a family—at the age of thirty-six it was time. And conception might prove easier if she wasn't rushing from pillar to post from the crack of dawn.

The likelihood of another florist taking over the business and keeping her on was slim—profits had been dropping for the last year. 'You'd better start looking for something else,' Manda had warned. 'If you find something, don't worry about working out your notice. I can wind the business down on my own. No probs.' So that meant she had to find something double quick if she was to be able to pay the rent on this flat.

The sound of the doorbell made her spirits lift. Cleo, her best friend since schooldays, had said she'd pop by this evening, bring a bottle of wine, and they could discuss her wedding plans. Milly was to be chief bridesmaid.

Glad that her friend was a couple of hours early—she'd mentioned nine as the most likely time—she flew down the narrow, carpetless staircase to let her in. And found she was staring at a complete stranger.

A drop dead handsome stranger.

An unexplained sensation quivered its way down her spine, intensifying as a shard of triumph glimmered briefly in the stranger's dark eyes and the sinfully sexy mouth curved in a smile that was definitely more predatory than friendly.

'The disguise doesn't fool me, Jilly, but it suits you—believe it or not.'

The deep voice was slightly accented; it made her toes curl. He obviously thought she was her glamorous twin, dressed in the sort of gear Jilly wouldn't be seen dead in—faded old jeans and woolly sweater, the trademark long beautiful hair cut to a boyish bob, and she shook her head, about to tell him he'd made an understandable mistake. But he forestalled her, striding past her, drawling crushingly, 'You should have known there was no place to hide. Lesson one—no one messes with me and mine. Lesson two—you pay for trying.'

Heavens! What had Jilly done now? The burning question went unspoken as he reached the foot of the dimly lit stairs and swung round to face her. Her breath caught, her heart hammered, speech was impossible for the moment because he looked so formidable.

Not an ounce of spare flesh on his impeccably suited six foot frame, broad shoulders, narrow waist and elegantly long legs. The dark hair, spangled with raindrops, was superbly cut, his features austerely sculpted but saved from coldness by a wickedly sensual mouth. And those eyes—rich dark chocolate with penetrating amber glints trained on her own green ones, which were wide with apprehension.

'My grandmother is already missing you. I will not have her upset. I told her you had to leave the villa because of a family crisis. You will stick to that story.' The long beautiful mouth tightened with distaste. 'Personally, I wouldn't let you within a mile of my home. But for Nonna's sake you will return to Tuscany with me tomorrow. You will take up your duties, continue to amuse and charm her but with one stricture—' he delivered chillingly '—there will be no more shopping trips in Florence on the pretext of refreshing her wardrobe and somehow persuading her to fill yours with designer gear. Understood?'

Not waiting for a reply, he drawled icily, his eyes threateningly narrowed on her now ashen face, 'The alternative is a spell in prison. I personally take care of my grandmother's finances. Did you think the large cash withdrawals would remain unnoticed? That I wouldn't make enquiries? The forged signatures on the cheques you presented are good enough for casual scrutiny by a clerk who recognised you as having accompanied the old lady who always used cash because she considered the use of plastic the devil's work. But not good enough to fool me. Or an expert brought in by the courts.'

Milly gasped and turned whiter. Shock had her feet rooted to the spot. Her heart was thumping so heavily she could hardly breathe. Her stomach seemed to be turning inside out and her head was reeling.

All through his hostile diatribe she'd been struggling to make sense of what he was saying, putting her initial and instinctive need to butt in and correct him on hold as the conviction that her identical twin was in trouble deepened, until the mention of prison, of fraud and theft made it impossible to let on that she wasn't the woman he was looking for.

Jilly was plainly in a horrible mess and until she could figure out what to do, how to protect her sister, she'd say nothing and hope she'd nodded off and this was a nightmare, not real.

But it was all too real.

He turned and headed for the door, his stride

lithe and totally assured, his shoulders straight and elegant. He opened the door, admitting damp air. 'I will collect you at six in the morning. Be ready. If you attempt to disappear again, be sure that I will find you. Be very sure of that.'

He turned then, his stunning eyes hard and cold. 'In the event of your non-compliance to my demands, I shall have no hesitation in hauling you through the courts and seeing you behind bars. My desire to protect my grandmother from the pain of discovering that the hired companion she had grown to trust, rely on and love was nothing more than a devious thief is strong. But even that has its limits.'

CHAPTER TWO

'HE CAN'T MAKE you *do* that!' Cleo howled, her perky face scarlet with outrage.

Secretly, Milly desperately wished she could agree with her. But she loved her twin and her conscience wouldn't let her wash her hands of her. When her friend had arrived, complete with samples of fabric, wedding magazines and a bottle of wine, she had still been sitting, stunned, on the draughty staircase.

And she'd let it all out, relaying every word the Italian had said and now, the wine poured, Cleo was glaring at her across the table. 'You must be crazy. I won't let you! Phone him and put him straight. Now. What's his name and where's he staying?'

Milly shrugged, fiddling abstractedly with the stem of her wineglass. 'How should I know? It would have given the game away if I'd asked his name, wouldn't it! He thinks I'm Jilly, his grandmother's companion. So I shouldn't need to ask his name! And, as for where he's staying, I didn't get the chance to ask since he didn't let me get a word in edgewise, and I was too shocked to even think of asking, even if he had. He just kept on threatening—'

'Which is exactly why you should tell him who you really are,' Cleo stressed. 'Have nothing more to do with him, let him go find the real Jilly. Let her pay for what she's done.'

Milly could understand her friend's strong misgivings, but, she said, 'I'm really worried about her. The guy who was here has a short fuse, that was glaringly obvious. If I tell him the truth and he has to go searching for Jilly all over again he'll quickly run out of patience and get the law involved. He looked and acted like the kind of guy who would get Interpol jumping and she'd be hunted down and dragged in front of a judge.' Her stomach twisted painfully at the thought and her voice shook as she repeated, 'I'm worried about her. She's always been headstrong but never dishonest. I'm as sure as I can be that there's been some ghastly mistake.'

Which earned her a sharp reply, 'You don't call it dishonest to persuade your mother to mortgage her home to the hilt, cash in that bond your father set up for a rainy day just before he died, get her to go in as an equal partner in that crackpot beauty salon business then do a runner when it went bust, leaving your mother with a mountain of debts, no home to call her own, just this grotty rented flat.'

Put like that it did sound, well, a bit selfish. Milly's clear green eyes clouded. But, to be fair to her twin, their mother had been only too glad to fall in with Jilly's plans if only to have her favourite daughter permanently home again. Jilly, the outgoing bubbly twin, able to charm the birds out of the trees, had always been everyone's favourite. She, Milly, had always been the quiet one, the home-body happy to be in the background, lacking her identical twin's glamour and drive, so she hadn't resented occupying second place. Not at all.

They'd been eighteen when Dad had died of a massive and totally unexpected heart attack, leaving his wife shattered and helpless.

Dear Arthur had always made all the decisions, handled all the finances, ruled his small family with a rod of iron. After his death Jilly had persuaded mum to finance a crash course to enable her to get her Beauty Specialists Diploma. It had meant living away from home and had taken almost every penny of mum's liquid savings. 'I'll pay every penny back when I'm earning loads, I promise. Will you do that for me, Ma? For my glittering future?'

Who could resist Jilly in cajoling mood? So it had fallen to her, Milly, to go to work for Manda, to take her father's place when it came to handling the family's dwindling finances, to orchestrate the necessary move from the spacious five-bedroom detached in the leafy countryside surrounding Ashton Lacey to a three bedroomed semi behind the cattle market.

When Jilly had briefly returned to the quiet market town with her diploma she had looked fantastic, lightly tanned courtesy of a sun-bed, her long blonde hair stylishly cut and glistening with subtle ash highlights, her make-up perfect, as was her figure encased in narrow white jeans and an emerald silk shirt that deepened the green of her eyes and made them look like glittering jewels.

She'd stayed two days, being waited on hand and foot by her captivated mother, until she'd left for London, imparting that she had a job interview lined up with a top flight beauty therapy clinic attached to a famous store and if Milly had felt envious she'd blanked out the unworthy emotion because her twin had what it took and she obviously didn't.

Jilly had got the job. No one had doubted that she would, but Milly and her mother had both missed the fizz she brought to the staid household. Her mother had become in turn tetchy or morose and rarely smiled and Milly, although she'd done her best, hadn't been able to take the place of the favourite missing daughter.

And then Jilly had returned and dropped her bombshell. 'I've jacked it in. I want to open my own salon here in Ashton Lacey. Why should I be a wage slave when I could rake in all the profits!'

'Where will the money come from?' Milly had wanted to know. 'It would cost a small fortune to set up.'

Jilly had turned her brittle smile on her. 'Trust you to be a wet blanket, sis.' Turning to her mother, her smile now honey-sweet, she said, 'You know what they say, Ma, you've got to speculate to accumulate. So this is how I see it—you could mortgage this house and cash in that bond thing Dad set up and you and I could go into partnership, fifty-fifty, or sixty-forty in your favour if you prefer. You'd never regret it. I forecast great things! After two years working for someone else I know the business inside out. We'll make money hand over fist—you'd never believe the profit margins! We could pay off the mortgage then sit back while the money rolls in. Say yes, Ma, and we'll go hunting for suitable premises to rent tomorrow.'

Ma had agreed, of course she had, her happiness that darling Jilly would be around permanently blinding her to the very real risks, and Milly could remember feeling like a no-account misery when she'd pointed out all the possible pitfalls.

The business had gone bankrupt within a couple of years. As Milly had tried to point out, Ashton Lacey wasn't ready for a glitzy state-of-the-art beauty salon. Drawing custom from a population mostly comprising the wives of small traders and scattered farmers had proved impossible and the few clients they'd had had rarely come a second time.

Everything had been sold to pay the creditors and Jilly hadn't hung around long enough to help them find somewhere to live—the rented flat above the butcher's—but had gone to Italy to seek her fortune.

To begin with there had been occasional postcards. She'd found work in Florence in an upmarket nightclub. Moved into a basement flat behind the Palazzo Vecchio, was meeting lots of interesting people, picking up the language and having loads of fun.

Sadly, she was not yet earning enough to be able to send money home to help pay off debts. She'd even given a phone number where she could be reached most late afternoons. Then, around eighteen months later, the final postcard,

'Wow! I think I've made it! I'm moving on. If I play my cards right—and I'll make sure I do—I'll be able to pay back every penny, Ma darling. With interest! I'll write again soon and give you a contact number.'

It had been the last they had heard of her.

'Jilly always meant to make things right, pay back everything Ma had lost,' Milly defended. 'She'd get these wild ideas and truly believe in them at the time, though how she imagined she'd make a small fortune working as a paid companion beggars belief.'

'Steal it, apparently,' Cleo put in drily, making Milly want to smack her.

'There's been a mistake. I know it.'

Cleo shook her head. 'It didn't sound like it from what that guy told you. She's obviously done another runner. I don't know why you insist on defending her.'

For a moment Milly couldn't speak. She was too angry. Her eyes flashed fire and the skin over her high cheekbones pinkened.

Then, reminding herself that Cleo was genuinely concerned for her, she took in a deep breath and offered, 'You don't understand the bond between twins. Why should you? But it goes deep, I promise. When we were growing up she always looked out for me. I got bullied at school, so she sorted them out. At home Dad could be…difficult. If I did something wrong like, oh, I don't know—like breaking something or tramping mud all over the floor—she'd take the blame and just stand there while he came down on her like a ton of bricks, bawled her out and sent her to her room or stopped her pocket money for a month. I love her and I owe her.'

'Sorry.' Cleo reached over and patted Milly's hand. 'Me and my big mouth! I just don't like the idea of you disappearing into the wilds of Tuscany with a man who obviously loathes you, or rather who he thinks you are. And what will he do when he finds out you've made a fool of him?'

'He won't,' Milly assured her with more conviction than she actually felt. 'We are identical. Jilly looks more glamorous because she knows how to dress for effect and how to use make-up. There's stuff of hers here that she left behind. She won't mind me borrowing it so, initially, he won't be able to tell the difference.' She took a healthy gulp of her forgotten wine. 'While he thinks I'm Jilly and I'm doing what I'm supposed to, she'll be safe from prosecution. And I guess even companions have time off. I'll use it to try and find her. She probably just walked out of the job because she got bored with dancing attendance on an old lady and there must have been some misunderstanding about the money. She won't have any idea that the old lady's grandson is out for her blood. When I find her she can go back and explain everything and sort the mess out.'

'And do you think you will? Find her.'

'I must.' Milly replied with intensity. 'At least I know now that she hasn't come to any harm. When we didn't hear anything after she left Florence we were desperately worried, though I tried to make light of it to Ma, stressing that Jilly had never been very good at keeping in touch, just a handful of postcards while she'd been working in London and even fewer when she'd been in Florence. But I was out of my head with worry. She hadn't said what her brilliant new money-making project was and you know how headstrong and reckless she can be—I thought anything could have happened to her.'

She relaxed back into her chair. 'At least I don't have to worry on that score. She was safely tucked up with some nice old lady!'

'Now—' she sprang to her feet, dredging up every ounce of courage she could find and holding on to it, ignoring the sick feeling in the pit of her stomach. 'Help me go through Jilly's things and tell me what I should take. We won't bother with her lingerie; I'll pack my own underwear and night things. He won't see that!'

'If I must.' Cleo followed her through to the third bedroom that had been set aside for Jilly's use. 'Though I'm miffed with you! You were going to be my chief bridesmaid, remember?'

Turning, Milly gave her a swift hug, promising confidently, 'The wedding's not for another three months—I'll be back long before then!'

But hours later, lying sleepless, she wondered. What if Jilly proved impossible to trace? She'd burned her bridges here. She'd phoned Manda at home and told her she'd found another job and wouldn't be in tomorrow. Had posted a cheque for three months' rent to her landlord, just about cleaning her account out but at least what few possessions she had would be safe.

And tomorrow she was leaving the country with an intimidating guy who thought she was the dregs of humanity and who would watch her like a hawk to make sure she didn't run off with the family silver.

She felt, quailing, as if her future no longer belonged to her.

CHAPTER THREE

MILLY KEPT HER aching, sleep-deprived eyes anxiously on the main double doors of the exclusive country hotel where the Italian had obviously spent the night. At least she now knew his name, which was a relief of sorts. When the driver had arrived at the flat, promptly at six, he'd asked, 'Miss Lee to meet Signor Saracino?'

And now the driver had entered the hotel and would emerge at any moment with Saracino and they would be driven to the airport. Her stomach rolled with dread and if it hadn't been for her need to find her sister and protect her from the intimidating Italian's misguided wrath she would have been out of this car like a shot and legging it down the long meandering shrub-bordered drive as if the devil himself was after her.

Which he would be, she sickeningly reminded herself. He hadn't impressed her as being a man who would give up easily. Give up full stop.

And then she saw him. And turned her head away abruptly, her heart pounding with the fleeting impression of immaculate strength, hard purpose and no mercy whatsoever. Her palms, knotted together on her lap, grew slick and she tried to pull a calming breath into her lungs but it stuck in her throat and almost choked her.

Could she hope to carry this off?

She had to. For Jilly's sake. She had no other option because if he saw through the deception he would be off after the real Jilly Lee faster than a hot knife through butter.

While the driver stowed Saracino's small amount of luggage in the boot alongside her bulky and battered suitcase and holdall the Italian merely gave her a cursory glance through the side window before wordlessly settling himself in the front passenger seat.

Relief that she'd been spared the ordeal of having him sit beside her in the rear of the car was sweet and she allowed herself the fleeting luxury of savouring it as the car purred back along the drive towards the main road. He probably couldn't bring himself to get close to her, or even look at her properly, for fear of contamination, which was a good omen for the future. Couldn't be better!

The more he kept his distance the safer she would be from discovery and she'd handle being a companion to someone who would naturally expect her to be au fait with the routine of their days somehow. Getting through check in without anyone noticing the slight difference in the name on the ticket and the one on her passport seemed another good omen.

But once they were at the airport, through security, he did look at her. Properly.

Dark eyes took on a cynical glint as they swept her from head to toe and Milly's stomach rolled over then tightened into a sickening knot. Forcing herself to lift her chin and meet those coldly disparaging eyes, she assured herself firmly that there was no way he could tell he was looking at the wrong twin.

Jilly's cream-coloured linen suit with its lapel-less fitted jacket and narrow knee-length skirt was classily eye-catching enough to fool him, especially since last night when she'd been wearing her usual boring everyday clothes he'd taken her for her twin—the short no-nonsense hairstyle, lack of make-up—all the things that had always marked her as being different from her sister.

Nevertheless she quaked in Jilly's bronze kitten heels when he delivered cuttingly, 'I'm glad to see you've toned down your act. Contrition? Somehow I don't think so. More likely to be sheer pig-headed annoyance at having been traced and hauled back to make reparation for your sins.'

She didn't know what he meant by that

'toning down' bit and watched with sickening fascination as broad shoulders lifted in a slight shrug which denoted that he couldn't care less either way. And then his strongly sculpted features hardened as he added, 'You will stick to the fiction that you were called away because of a family crisis, apologise for not calling my grandmother during your absence and continue to please her with your company for as long as you are needed. The money you stole can be taken as future wages; you will receive no further payments from me. Is that understood?'

Dry mouthed, Milly nodded speechlessly, her flagging spirits taking a further nose-dive. She would work for him but would receive no pay!

She couldn't use her debit card because, after forking out for that advance rent payment her account was as good as bare. And relying on her seldom used credit card was out of the question. She couldn't afford to get into debt. Penniless apart from a couple of five pound notes and the loose change in her purse, her plan for travelling around on her days off—provided she was allowed such a luxury—to try and trace her twin bit the dust.

Trying not to let her agitation show, to sound as wryly confident as Jilly would have done in similar circumstances, she asked, 'Will I still have time off? Or will I be locked in my room when your grandmother doesn't need me, Signor Saracino?'

One strongly arched dark brow lifted in marked contempt as he countered, 'So formal. I recall a much more intimate mode of address when you came to my bed.'

He swung away as their flight was called, leaving Milly to stagger in his wake, too shell shocked to notice that he hadn't answered her question.

Cocooned in the luxury of first class, Milly's mind was racing. A sideways glance showed her his impressive profile bent over a file he'd taken from his briefcase, the pen held in long finely made tanned fingers stabbing notes into the margins of the closely typed pages.

She looked quickly away, her heart fluttering as a strange sensation gathered in the pit of her stomach. Jilly and the Italian had been lovers.

So why had that announcement really shocked her? Her sister had had affairs before.

'Things' she'd called them. 'I'm having this thing with—whoever.' None of them had lasted longer than a month or two. Jilly had always been restless, easily bored.

Had it been different this time? Had Jilly fallen in love with the savagely handsome Italian? Milly, her cheeks growing greatly overheated, could easily understand that. He was drop-dead-gorgeous, magnetic. Even she, on the receiving end of his icy menace, could recognise that. In the role of sexy seducer he would be dynamite! Totally irresistible!

Had her sister believed Saracino loved her in return? Had she expected marriage? Been sublimely confident of it? That would explain the wild promise that if she played her cards right she would be able to pay Ma back with interest. Everything about him spoke of wealth and standing and it would explain why the lively, flamboyant Jilly had uncharacteristically taken the post of humble companion to an old lady. Just to be near the man she loved and hoped to marry, to be available.

And had she left secretly, nursing a broken heart, when she'd discovered that marrying her was the last thing on his mind?

She wouldn't know for sure until she found her twin. But the scenario seemed likely given the information on that final postcard from Florence and what she knew of the callous yet handsome man at her side.

Hating to think of her sister in trouble— hounded by this cold-hearted devil because of some mistake—and hurting because he'd broken her heart she gritted her teeth and vowed to find Jilly and clear her name. Her twin had always looked out for her, had taken her part when they'd been growing up.

She was more determined than ever to repay that debt.

Milly woke when he prodded her. 'Fasten your seat belt; we're about to land.'

Hating his tone, contempt tinged with searing impatience, she groggily complied. She hadn't thought she'd ever sleep again, at least not in his spiky company, but last night's deprivation had caught up with her. Smothering yawns, she felt at a total disadvantage while she followed where he led and it wasn't until they were well away from Pisa airport and driving along the labyrinthine white Tuscan lanes that he spoke to her, although she had much to her discomfit, been on the receiving end of quite a few penetrating sideways glances she'd felt rather than actually met.

'For some reason Nonna thinks the sun

shines out of you,' he imparted drily. 'Since your disappearance she has been fretting. You will do and say nothing to upset her. Is that clear?'

'Perfectly.'

Again that swift censorious sideways glance. 'Don't slouch! You look as though you're being driven to the gallows! You should be thanking the patron saint of sinners that you've got off so lightly.' His voice tightened. 'If it weren't for Nonna's fondness for you then, believe me, you'd be in handcuffs right now!'

Milly dragged in a deep, shuddering breath. How she stopped herself from reaching over and strangling the hateful man she would never know! A scarlet flush of rage flooded her delicate features. If Jilly were in her place, the object of his withering contempt, she would fall out of love with him faster than she could draw breath.

She couldn't trust herself to answer his scathing comments without giving the game away but, mindful of his scornful criticism, she sat up straighter.

In any other circumstances she would be enjoying riding in this open-topped racy sports car through the sun-soaked Tuscan scenery, through the patchwork landscape of vineyards and stately avenues of cypresses, orchards of lemon trees and distant craggy outcrops of rock.

As it was she was getting more wound up and edgy with every mile that passed and when a bend in the narrow road revealed a paved driveway flanked by elegant wrought iron gates and the imposing stone villa beyond she felt as if she were about to splinter with tension.

Would she make it through the acid test, her meeting with Saracino's grandmother, without giving herself away? Back in England she had told herself that her identical physical appearance, the wearing of her twin's clothes, was all she needed to stop the Italian searching for the real Jilly and having her charged with fraud and goodness only knew what else. But here the possible pitfalls loomed very large indeed.

Telling herself to watch her step at all times, she exited the car as the grim faced Italian pulled to a halt in front of the massive iron-studded open double doors and watched as he handed the car keys to a wiry little man who had appeared out of nowhere then turned to her.

'Stefano will take your cases to your room. Wait in the hall while I go to prepare Nonna for your return.'

No way!

Outwardly compliant, Milly preceded him into the coolness of the marble paved reception hall, then watched as Saracino, handsome as all-get-out in the superbly styled light grey suit that drew attention to his broad back, narrow hips and long, elegantly strong legs, walked purposefully towards one of the gleaming, intricately carved doors that led off this huge space.

Then she dragged in a deep breath and scampered after Stefano as he mounted the sweeping staircase, congratulating herself on disregarding the boss's orders and discovering where Jilly's room was and avoiding the ignominy of pretending a short-term memory loss and having to confess to forgetting which room was hers!

Concentrating hard, she followed Stefano as he turned left where the magnificent staircase branched, down a panelled corridor hung with portraits and landscapes in heavy gilded frames, counting doors to left and right.

First hurdle over! It was the only positive thought she'd had since leaving England when Stefano opened the third door on the right. Smartly suppressing the instinctive cry of delight, she entered the room that had been supposedly hers for the last few months, the most beautiful room she had ever seen with its soft ivory-coloured carpet, panelled walls colour-washed in the same shade, gleaming antique furniture and the most opulent tester bed she had ever laid eyes on, layers of white lace topped by a satin quilt in a lovely shade of dusky rose, the whole enclosed with gauzy drapes. Not to mention the magnificent vaulted wooden ceiling, painted with swags of flowers, cherubs and exotic birds.

Placing her luggage on the low chest at the foot of the bed, Stefano said in passable English, 'Not to use the smart *valigia* the Signora buy for you?'

As his glance rested on the old hold-all and shamefully battered suitcase into which she had stuffed Jilly's lovely clothes she understood his meaning, found a smile and invented rapidly, 'I didn't want it to get scuffed; I wanted it to stay smart.'

Which earned her a beam of approval and the self-congratulatory thought that so far she was doing just fine. Which lasted precisely five seconds, the time it took for Stefano to exit and for her to realise that she was facing her reflection in a full length pier glass.

Staring at herself, she simply couldn't believe Saracino hadn't seen through the deception! True, feature for feature, she and Jilly were identical, but where her twin walked and held herself with sublime confidence, she drooped!

Hastily hauling her shoulders back, she pushed her fringe out of her eyes. Eyes innocent of any artifice. Unfortunately Jilly hadn't left any of her cosmetics behind, just the clothes she'd worn a couple of times and grown tired of. So Milly had had to do the best she could with her usual moisturiser and rarely used rose-pink lipstick. Totally different from the trade mark scarlet pout, heavily darkened lashes and expertly applied foundation, eye shadow and blusher.

No wonder Saracino had made that scathing remark about toning down her act!

She was going to have to try harder! Make herself act, walk and talk like her sister, because if she didn't then sooner or later—probably sooner—she would be rumbled. The thought terrified her so much that she felt nauseous as she made her way back to the huge hall.

Where Saracino was waiting, pacing, and clearly not pleased.

His nostrils flared, dark eyes shooting a dire warning at her, he bit out, 'I told you to wait here.'

Inwardly quailing, Milly straightened her spine. Never mind how Jilly would have reacted to this ogre in the guise of an Adonis, she, Milly, wasn't going to be spoken to as if she were a dim-witted form of low-life. 'So you did.' Proud of her dulcet tone, achieved with great self-control, she added serenely, 'But I needed the bathroom. Now I will make my apologies to Nonna.'

'She is not your grandmother. I won't have a creature like you presuming family connections!' The sensual mouth compressed with distaste as he took her arm in ungentle fingers. 'You will address her as Filomena, as you always have done, and as Signora Saracino when speaking to the staff on her behalf.'

Little did he know it but because of her slip of the tongue he was being a great help. This thought buoyed her a little as he practically frog-marched her through an intricately carved door that led into a sitting room of beautiful proportions.

Tall windows lay open to an arcaded stone veranda admitting the soft spring light that gleamed back from gilded looking glasses and exquisite inlaid furniture. But Milly's attention wasn't for the obvious grandeur of the surroundings, it was all for the beaming elderly mauve-clad lady seated in a throne-like chair that dwarfed her frail body, both hands held out in welcome.

'Jilly—naughty girl! Running away without a word!' The warmth of the tone and the smile that went with it robbed her words of any sting. 'Come, let me look at you.'

Unnervingly conscious of a pair of hard black eyes boring into the back of her head, Milly went forward on legs that felt like wet cotton wool, uncomfortably aware that if she put a foot wrong Filomena Saracino would see right through her and out her as the imposter she was.

Frail fingers clasped her own and the warmth of affection flooded through Milly and made her want to weep because the warmth wasn't for her but for her charismatic sister. Jilly, the golden girl, only had to turn on that effortless charm of hers to have the recipient eating out of her beautifully manicured hands.

'You've cut off all your hair; why did you do that, child?'

Disconcertingly—her sister was a total stranger to blushes—Milly felt her face flood with colour. She hated having to lie to this patently nice old lady. She pulled a breath into her suddenly oxygen-starved lungs and managed, 'With the hot weather coming I thought it would be cooler,' and heard behind her a cynical huff of breath. Saracino. He believed she'd done it to try to alter her appearance; he'd said as much at their first meeting.

'Very practical.' The silvery head was tipped assessingly, the faded eyes lively, 'It suits you. You look younger; don't you think so, Cesare?'

Which elicited no response, but Milly knew

his first name now and that was one more brick in the edifice of deception she was building up—a necessary deception, she hastily reassured herself, as distaste for the part she was playing flooded her conscience.

The old lady released her hands and prompted gently, 'Now pull up a chair and tell me about the family crisis that took you away from me.'

Silently Cesare placed a delicate upright chair a little to the side and a little in front of where his grandmother was sitting, then took himself across the room to lean against the huge marble fire surround, one arm draped over the top, feet crossed at the ankles.

He might appear relaxed but he wasn't. Those dark hostile eyes didn't leave her for a single moment, Milly noted sinkingly as she sat on the chair he had provided and tugged the hem of her narrow skirt more demurely over her knees. He was watching her like a hawk to make sure she didn't do or say anything to upset his grandmother or leap up and snatch the rope of pearls from around the old lady's throat and make a run for it, she thought with rising hysteria.

'It must have been important,' Filomena probed. 'For you to leave without saying goodbye, or phone me later to tell me what was happening.' Her voice trembled slightly. 'I really missed you. The days seemed so long and dull without you to brighten them for me.' The eyes that had seemed so lively on her arrival now dulled. 'Would you have come back if Cesare hadn't gone to England to find you?'

A lump the size of a small planet formed at the base of her throat and from the opposite side of the room Cesare put in, as smooth and deadly as black ice, 'Don't upset yourself, Nonna. I know Jilly can put your mind at rest.' Dark eyes narrowed on her troubled face and she heard the threat behind his seemingly bland tone.

'Can't you, Jilly?

CHAPTER FOUR

SUDDENLY MILLY COULD hear herself breathing. Shallow and too rapid. The soft calling of the doves in the flower-decked courtyard she could glimpse beyond the stone arcade seemed preternaturally loud in the ear-tingling silence that awaited her response.

She swallowed heavily and stared at her short no-nonsense fingernails, then clenched her fists to hide them out of sight of querying eyes because Jilly wouldn't be seen dead without long, perfectly manicured nails.

Inventing an important crisis was completely impossible. Piling lie on unnecessary lie was utterly distasteful. Besides, of late hadn't there been many all too real crises in her life—the bruising advent of Cesare Saracino, mislaying her sister, losing her mother?

The death of her mother just over a month ago had been the absolute worst. The reminder of that dreadful day was rawly, painfully devastating and her voice shook with the emotion she couldn't hide as she whispered, 'My mother died. It was very sudden.' And at times it seemed as if it had happened only yesterday.

Her eyes flooded. The loss still hurt dreadfully, compounded by the fact that she had had no means of contacting Jilly and having her come home for the funeral to give her support and to pay her respects to the mother who had doted on her.

A beat of silence followed the statement, then, 'Oh my dear! How sad for you. What a terrible shock.' Filomena leant forward and took both her hands again, her eyes full of sympathy. 'You make me so very ashamed of my grumbles. Of course you would have been too distraught—and harried with all the arrangements to even think about me, let alone phoning or writing to let me know what was happening. I understand perfectly. Forgive me for doubting your intention to return.'

Choking back a sob, it was all Milly could do to manage a husky, 'Of course.'

The pressure of the frail fingers increased as Filomena angled a sharp look in her grandson's direction. 'I trust Cesare didn't pressure you into returning before you were ready?'

There was no honest disclaimer Milly could give to that and, thankfully, the need to reply was obviated by the elderly lady saying, 'I know you said your little sister is very practical and dull, without a sensitive or imaginative thought in her head, but will she be all right on her own? She must be feeling lonely without you, especially during this time of family mourning.'

'She's fine,' Milly said hollowly and felt her cheeks flame with discomfiture. That Jilly should describe her as being her little sister she could just about understand. To Jilly it must have felt that way. Her twin had always been the leader, she the follower. But practical and dull with no imagination or sensitivity—was that how Jilly really saw her? It hurt.

Cesare had moved to stand behind his grandmother's chair and the look he glued on her was definitely speculative. Which somehow made everything ten times worse.

The old lady turned her head briefly towards him then turned back again to smile at Milly. 'We will invite your sister for a holiday. Next month? Before the weather gets too hot—May here is such a lovely month. A holiday will be good for you both and I shall enjoy having two young things to keep me company.'

Mistaking the unwitting look of horror on Milly's face for something else entirely her mouth curved impishly. 'I won't expect you both to dance attendance on me all the time, of course. You will have the use of one of the cars to take her sightseeing and shopping. Now, if you'll excuse me, I shall take my usual rest before dinner so why don't you phone home and let your sister know you have arrived safely, and mention the offer of a holiday—do your best to persuade her? Then you must also rest after your journey and we'll see each other again at dinner.'

Filomena got stiffly to her feet and Cesare handed her a walking cane. Then Milly noted sinkingly that his strong lean face was turned to her, those dark penetrating eyes burning into her apprehensive green ones as he addressed her in a torrent of Italian.

Feeling sick with nerves, Milly bit into the soft underside of her bottom lip, her brain turning dizzily as it scrambled to recall what Jilly had written on one of those postcards.

That she was picking up the language!

Was the deception to be uncovered so soon, so easily? There was a thumping silence as she failed to respond to what it was he'd been saying to her.

'Now, Cesare.' Unwittingly Filomena came to her rescue. 'You know the rules. English only!'

'Of course, Nonna. I apologise.' Cesare dipped his dark head and Milly was sure a hard smile tugged at the corners of his handsome mouth. 'I shall reframe my question in perfect English,' he delivered silkily, eyes as cold as the Arctic winter holding hers. 'Would Jilly like to give me her home number? I can dial it for her as I know the correct international code.'

'That won't be necessary,' Milly returned thinly, and smiled for Filomena. 'I'll see you to your room before I phone home.' She shot Cesare a challenging glance. 'Milly won't have left work yet. And I expect she'll need to do some grocery shopping before she heads home.'

She had no intention of making that point-less call and with the feeling that she had survived somehow, had avoided quite a few pitfalls—even if the survival had relied more on luck than judgement—she accompanied the elderly lady to her ground floor suite, saw her settled and finally left with the promise that, yes, she would herself rest before dinner.

Thanks to her earlier foresight she found the room that had been Jilly's with no trouble at all and sat on the edge of the huge, opulent bed and lowered her bright head to her hands.

Back in England, anxious to save her twin from being treated like a criminal, hauled before a judge to answer to charges she was surely innocent of, she had blithely believed that this deception was necessary if only to give her the time to try and trace her missing sister, put her in the picture and get her to clear everything up.

She hadn't wanted the cold-hearted Cesare to find her first, refuse to listen to anything she said in her own defence and have her clapped in irons before she could draw breath.

She still didn't. Of course she didn't! But the deception was making her feel ill and desperately ashamed of herself. Not on Cesare's account, that was for sure! He was the brute who had broken her sister's heart, bedded her, led her to believe he would marry her. Then dumped her. At least everything pointed that way. Why else would Jilly have disappeared?

But deceiving a lovely, kindly old lady was despicable. It was pricking her conscience like a red-hot poker! She couldn't do it.

She was going to have to come clean.

Cesare ended the second call and swivelled his chair away from the leather-topped desk so that he could face the bank of tall windows that overlooked the expanse of emerald-green lawns that swept uninterrupted to the stone perimeter wall.

Shadows were lengthening as the sun sank towards the horizon and beyond the wall he could see the misty amethyst of distant hills, the nearest terraced and surrounded by clusters of ochre-walled houses and farmsteads.

His strongly angled brows drew down darkly as he dragged in a huff of breath and swooped back from the view that always calmed him and faced his desk again, one lean tanned hand reaching for an address book.

The enigma he was tussling with was his grandmother's wretched thieving companion. Lots of things about Jilly Lee didn't sit right.

Her demeanour was quiet, almost subdued. Instead of in-your-face bright and bubbly. Short, unvarnished fingernails, the lack of beauty-salon-glossy make-up.

All of which could be put down to the fact that the bounce had been knocked out of her when he'd caught up with her and forced her to come back and work without remuneration until the amount she had stolen had been repaid. Plus, she would be on a low following the death of her mother. No puzzle there. Her grief had been genuine, the emotion real and raw.

Yet he had always been an astute judge of character and early on he had decided that Jilly Lee was completely shallow, incapable of an emotion that wasn't entirely self-centred.

And then again—he had instant recall of her look of mystification when he'd addressed her in Italian. Jilly Lee was pretty near fluent.

True, English only was Nonna's strict rule and it had paid off because she was now conversing with ease and the challenge to brush up on the language had been good for her, had given her a real interest.

But her companion had always used Italian when speaking with the staff and when she was alone with him—a situation she had contrived with tedious regularity.

So why the seeming lack of comprehension when he'd simply asked for a phone number? Something didn't sit right.

His mouth compressed, he leafed through the address book until he found the number he wanted. There were ways to get to the bottom of the enigma. Already he had put two investigators on the case. The one in England who had initially found Jilly Lee's family's home address, the other here to follow a possible Italian trail.

There was something he could do himself

to get to the bottom of what was needling him. But he couldn't do it here.

He drew the phone towards him, lifted the receiver and punched in numbers.

'Contessa—'

The dining room was magnificent but Milly couldn't exclaim over the wonders of the painted ceiling, decorated with garlands of flowers, fruits and impish putti, or the two fantastic Venetian chandeliers above the long, highly polished table because as Jilly she would know the interior of the villa inside out.

And she was in no real state to properly appreciate any of it, the room, the food served on delicate porcelain plates, the heavy silver flatware, the wine—a different one for each course—in exquisite crystal glasses.

Because.

She was riven with guilt over the deception. Had made up her mind to confess all to Filomena. But not while that handsome, cynical devil was around. His wrath at having been fooled would be shattering and his willingness to listen to her defence of her twin non existent.

But she was sure Filomena would listen. The old lady, trigged out in violet silk with diamonds at her throat was chattering nineteen to the dozen. Cesare remarked laconically, 'You're in good form this evening, Nonna.' The old lady lifted her glass and replied, 'That is because my dear Jilly is with me again, to keep me entertained and stop me from expiring from tedium.'

'Which role I am obviously unable to fill,' Cesare returned with wry fondness.

'Of course!' The faded eyes twinkled. 'Girl-talk is a stranger to you! Besides—' she dipped her spoon into her zabaglione with obvious relish '—you are so often away. Although I have noticed—' again the twinkle this time accompanied by a tiny knowing smile '—that since Jilly joined us you have rarely left the villa.'

The interchange made Milly wonder if

Filomena had guessed that the two had become lovers and had silently condoned it, hoping perhaps—as Jilly must have done—that marriage was on the cards.

Which reinforced her opinion that Filomena would listen to her, side with her in defence of her missing twin; she was genuinely very fond of her. Jilly had obviously done what she did best, had used her charm until the recipient was eating out of her pretty hands. A knack, Milly ruefully reminded herself, that she singularly lacked.

Yes, Filomena would roundly deny that Jilly had forged those cheques, would explain that she had signed them herself when she hadn't been feeling on top form, which would be why the signatures had raised suspicions.

Emboldened by that possible explanation, she raised her eyes and found Cesare's eyes on her, focused with an intensity that made her blood run cold and then hot. Very hot. The smile that played around the edges of his mouth was wilfully sinful and it did awful things to her.

Her stomach tightened then flipped, just as it had done earlier when he'd come to her room.

He'd entered after a perfunctory knock and she'd been standing there in her plain un-Jilly-like undies. Her face flaming, she'd grabbed her sister's black silk sheath from where she'd laid it ready on the bed and held it in front of her. Feeling sick with embarrassment, she spilled out, 'What do you want?'

Leaning with casual grace against the door frame he looked magnificent. All dark and brooding and unnervingly sexy in his cream dinner jacket and narrow black trousers. No wonder Jilly had fallen hook line and sinker for the heartless brute, was her near hysterical thought as she clasped the black dress infront of her as if it were body armour.

'To remind you that we dine early, at seven-thirty, for my grandmother's sake—in case you'd forgotten. You are already late.' Delivered with extreme dryness.

'Of course I hadn't forgotten,' she denied.

How could she forget something she hadn't known? 'I fell asleep,' she excused untruthfully, unable to tell him that she'd spent ages going over the room here and in the luxurious *en suite* bathroom, opening cupboards and drawers to see if Jilly had left anything behind that would tell her that her sister had meant to return when she'd recovered from the worst effects of a broken heart and shattered dreams.

She had found nothing, not even a hairpin. Disconsolately she'd run a bath and had soaked for an hour, then selected the black dress from amongst the things one of the staff must have unpacked, and had been getting ready to dress and go down to Filomena's room and tell her everything.

'I'll be even later if you don't leave so I can get dressed,' Milly said tightly, willing him to take his desperately unnerving presence away.

'I'll wait.' Posting his intention, Cesare sauntered further into the room and Milly, her chin set at a stubborn angle, her eyes glittering with loathing, backed out and slammed the bathroom door behind her.

Who the hell did he think he was? she raged internally. Bang went her intention to explain everything to his unsuspecting grandmother before they all had to sit through dinner together.

Struggling into the dress, she did her best to calm down. In her role as Filomena's companion she would get loads of time alone with her tomorrow. She had wanted to get everything off her chest right now, but it would just have to wait.

And at least he hadn't figured out that she wasn't the real Jilly. If he had she would have been thrown out of the villa at the speed of light, the doors locked and barred behind her and her intentions to confess to Filomena and get her on side vanishing like a puff of smoke in a hurricane.

Facing one of the mirrored walls Milly noted that her face had gone scarlet from the combined effects of temper, frustration and her inability to pull the back zip all the way up.

And then, to her huge annoyance, Cesare's reflection appeared behind her. 'Allow me.' In one concise movement he had the zip in place, the backs of his fingers brushing against skin that suddenly felt unbearably sensitised. 'I thought you might have died in here.' His mouth curved in sardonic humour and, Milly translated huffily, he thought she might have jumped out of the window with the family silver concealed in her underwear!

His reflected eyes, partially veiled by his thick dark lashes, swept slowly down her body and Milly's insides squirmed, her face reddening again. The dress fitted like a second skin. Jilly had always worn her clothes on the tight side. 'If you've got it, flaunt it!' Whereas she had always preferred not to draw attention to her curvy hips, tiny waist and the generous breasts that were even now humiliating her by peaking, thrusting unashamedly against the fine silk barrier of the dress.

She didn't know what had come over her to make her body respond this way. The stress of the situation, she guessed, frustrated because she seemed to have no control over her own body.

Moving briskly to one side, she turned and marched back into the bedroom, pushed her feet into a pair of Jilly's heels and followed him out into the corridor and now here they were, the ongoing stress of having to pretend to eat and respond to Filomena's chatter thankfully coming to an end and he was leaning back in his chair, cradling his wine-glass in one lean, tanned hand, the picture of smooth sophistication.

Cesare had made little contribution to the conversation, just watched her from the depths of those clever eyes, making her wish the floor would open like a trapdoor and swallow her up, but when a stout black-clad woman entered with a dark-haired slip of a girl in close attendance, Filomena stood. 'No coffee for me, Rosa. I think I will retire early after today's excitement.' Cesare stood too and settled his grandmother back in her chair.

'Stay a moment. I have a surprise for you.'

'A nice one?' Her smile was teasing.

'I believe you'll think so,' he replied fondly. 'Amalia is coming to see you tomorrow. She plans on staying for at least two weeks. Apparently, she's spent the last six months in virtual hiding recovering from her latest facelift and various nips and tucks.'

'Amalia! How splendid!' Pleasure shone from the old lady's eyes. She smiled for Milly. 'The Contessa di Moroschini is my oldest friend and so outrageous! I know you will enjoy her!'

'That's something I'd like to talk to you about, Nonna.'

He turned to Milly, the gentle warmth that always transformed his harsh features when talking to his grandmother disappearing like water down a plughole. 'As Amalia will be here to keep you company and amused with her latest and possibly near-scandalous doings, I thought I'd steal your companion for a week—take her to the island and allow her to rest and recover from her recent bereavement.' He turned back to Filomena and Milly, too shocked to speak, felt a peculiar shudder race down her spine.

'That's if you approve, Nonna?'

'A splendid idea!' Satisfaction wreathed Filomena's features as she again got to her feet and Milly decided that her guess had been right. Signora Saracino knew about her grandson's affair with Jilly and hoped it would have a happy ending. She would have to be disabused at some time, told that her so-perfect grandson had cruelly given Jilly the elbow, had made her fly from the villa with a broken heart. But now? When she was so happy at the prospect of a visit from an old friend?

Assaulted by violently conflicting emotions, torn between coming clean and spoiling the old lady's time with a much loved friend and carrying on the deception for a while longer and trying, somehow, to trace her sister, Milly also rose to her feet.

'I'll come with you.'

'Certainly not!' Filomena was already heading towards the door as the coffee things were laid out and the young maid cleared the table. 'I manage perfectly well. Enjoy your coffee and discuss your plans for the island.'

Her retreat blocked, Milly subsided back in her seat and wearily accepted the coffee Cesare had poured for her and bit back the instinctive words that would tell him she had no intention of going anywhere with him.

The real Jilly surely would have jumped at what would appear to be a chance of reconciliation. The opportunity to convince him that she hadn't forged those cheques.

Not having a clue as to how to play it, she sat back and left the initiative to him, merely swallowing sickly when he drained his cup, setting it back on its saucer as he got elegantly to his feet and told her, 'Be ready to leave at six-thirty,' and strode from the room.

Milly shuddered. She felt sick. Stuck on an island with him. No chance to try to trace her sister. No time now to get Filomena on side, either. Alone with him, he'd no doubt speak Italian to her and the cat would be out of the bag with a vengeance.

He'd know she wasn't Jilly.

And what he'd do then didn't bear thinking about!

CHAPTER FIVE

ENIGMA SOLVED!

Everything neatly explained, from her look of total incomprehension when he'd addressed her in Italian to her flustered attempts to cover herself when he'd walked into her room and found her in her underwear. The Jilly he knew would have displayed no such modesty.

Inwardly on a high of triumph, Cesare landed the helicopter on the specially constructed pad on the west side of the privately owned island, the rocky side that looked out over the azure sea to the lushly forested hills of Elba on the horizon.

Waiting for the rotors to come to a standstill, he angled himself into his seat and studied his passenger through narrowed, luxuriantly veiled eyes.

Lying, cheating, devious minx! He wondered idly how she thought she would get away with it and what her motive had been in the first place, then dismissed the consideration as unimportant.

Two could play that game and he'd make a better fist of it than she had.

She was staring ahead, her shoulders rigid beneath the silky blue top she was wearing above cropped, narrow fitting white jeans. She hadn't said a word since they'd left the villa, not even to ask where he was taking her, her lush mouth downturned like a sulky teenager, the only indication that anything was seriously amiss being the stark apprehension in those deep emerald eyes.

He could understand the apprehension. She was afraid of being found out. As well she might be; she was on decidedly shaky ground and must know it.

When he'd taken that call from the English

agent back there on the mainland airstrip, he'd been icily furious but not riven by surprise. He'd been puzzled ever since he'd escorted Nonna's absconding companion back to the villa and the flare of triumph over running the devious little thief to earth had died down sufficiently to let him see clearly.

The agent had made short work of discovering that there were two of them.

Jilly Lee and Milly Lee.

Identical twins.

His overriding imperative had been to wash his hands of the imposter, give her a well-deserved tongue lashing then walk away, leaving her standing on the airstrip, head back to the villa letting her find her own way back to England as best she could.

But in the space of time it took him to draw breath common sense had overcome his icy fury that she had believed she could make a fool of him—and, even worse, deceive his beloved grandmother.

To return to the villa now and explain everything to Nonna would be to deal her a severe blow. He couldn't do it. Not yet. It would ruin the happiness she was currently enjoying. The company of her old friend—who hadn't needed much in the way of pressure to agree to the last minute invitation to visit—and secure in the knowledge that her vibrant young companion was back in harness, her matchmaking tendencies surfacing again in her delight at his suggestion that he whisk her companion away to the island.

Nonna was old, she was frail and he loved her. Let her be happy for a little while longer.

His original intention to use the time on the island to solve the puzzle himself was now redundant. But he could amuse himself at her expense—she owed him a little light entertainment—and when she least expected it he would hit her with the fact that he knew the truth and hope to shock her sister's whereabouts from her, assuming the Italian and English agents had drawn a blank.

'You can get out now.' Softly spoken, his

condemning eyes on her delightful profile as he tried to read what went on inside that devious head.

The sisters were identical in face and body but this one—Milly—had an air of softness, almost vulnerability, about her that the other patently lacked. With her short blonde hair trailing soft tendrils against her tender nape and those startlingly green eyes she looked almost childlike. But there was nothing childlike about the full, pert breasts, tiny waist and luscious hips.

Gorgeous on the outside but inside they were, both of them, bent as corkscrews—she had to be just as devious and self serving as her much more in-your-face twin.

She gave no response, just the merest dip of her head to acknowledge she had heard him, her hands eventually straying with slow reluctance to the heavy-duty clasp of her seat belt.

Scared witless? As she had every right to be. Expecting him to bombard her with Italian, force her to confess she didn't understand a word of the language and reveal her true identity. She would be quaking in her shoes, waiting for the axe to fall.

His smile was self-admittedly victorious as his feet touched the ground. He would gently erase the fear, lull her into a false sense of security. And then hit her with his knowledge. Not exactly ethical, he conceded, but *Dio!* Nobody treated Nonna like a cash cow or a dupe and got away with it—not while he had breath in his body!

It felt as though all the ants in the world were charging up and down her spine wearing spiked boots, Milly decided feverishly. In sickening mental turmoil, she watched as Cesare lifted down her old suitcase and shouldered his own rucksack. Reaching down for her case, he set off up the stony track at speed, leaving Milly with no option but to follow.

She had no idea why he had brought her here. Whatever his reason, it didn't augur well for her, she acknowledged edgily. It certainly wasn't for the good of her health!

He thought she was a thief, a common con-woman, and she, in her role as Jilly, hadn't denied it and sought to clear her name as her maligned sister most surely would have done. She had just gone along with his dictates, seeing it as the only way to keep her sister out of his vindictive clutches and the cold hands of the law.

But she had the terrifying feeling that the deception would soon be discovered, laid bare before his contemptuous gaze. And then the hunt for the real Jilly Lee would be back on with a vengeance.

It wouldn't take long. All he had to do was start conversing in Italian. Without his grand-mother's rules there was no reason why he shouldn't use his native language and expect her to understand most, if not all, of it.

Knowing she had failed miserably and done her sister's cause no good at all she was unable to concentrate on where she was going when her foot hit a rock and, emitting a sharp cry of alarm, she fell flat on her face and lay spreadeagled in the growing heat of the sun. Winded, humiliated, short moments later she felt herself lifted to her feet by two strong hands and her eyes sparkled like fine jewels with unshed tears of chagrin.

'Are you hurt?'

Milly gulped for much needed oxygen and shook her head. Two displaced tears trickled down her pale-with-shock cheeks. He actually sounded as if he cared, his eyes narrowing with what looked suspiciously like concern as his gaze swept down the length of her shaken body.

His hands were on her slender shoulders now. They felt reassuring, comforting. She had the insane impulse to move closer to that strong, lean body, lay her troubled head against his broad chest and seek solace.

Hurriedly, she brushed the wimpy tears away and with them the weak need to be held by him. He was her sister's enemy; therefore he was her enemy too.

In similar circumstances Jilly would swear like a trooper, brush herself down and make a joke of it. In the impersonation stakes she wasn't doing too well.

She was going to have to try harder. Much harder. At least until he discovered that she wasn't who she was pretending to be.

'I'm fine.' She forced a smile. 'I wasn't looking where I was going.' She lifted her chin, wondering what Jilly would say next, and hit on, 'How much further? Isn't there any transport on the island?'

Her sister hadn't been known to walk if she could take a cab and rarely put herself in a situation where there wasn't one within hailing distance. But at her most Jilly-like comment to date Cesare's wickedly sexy mouth turned down at one corner as he drawled, 'There is nothing on the island but one stone cottage. No people, no roads and no bright lights.

His hands dropped from her shoulders and he turned away, striding along the rough track to where he'd dropped the luggage, then waited until she joined him. 'My father had it built when he bought the island many years ago. By all accounts he was a workaholic and came here at least once a year to recharge his batteries.'

'You must have happy memories of childhood holidays,' Milly responded to his totally unexpected mention of anything remotely personal, trying to act as normally as possible under difficult circumstances, doing her level best not to get too het up over the possibility of him leaving her here with no way of returning to the mainland once her deception had been uncovered. She certainly wouldn't put that kind of action past him!

For a moment she thought he wouldn't respond to her innocuous remark. She glanced up at his tanned, extravagantly handsome features and saw his mouth tighten with what she could only translate as scorn. 'My mother never came here. She was a metropolitan creature. My father brought his mistresses here, he didn't want me around. I only learned of the existence of this hideaway after his death.'

Biting back instinctive words of sympathy because she knew he wouldn't want them, Milly concentrated on getting up the increasingly steep track that traversed the sun-baked hillside where herbs and wild flowers merged their perfume with the tang of the sea and the scent of the pines she could see ahead of them. Breathless with heat and effort—neither of which seemed to affect him in the slightest—her mind was busy.

If his father had taken mistresses openly enough for him to know about them then that would explain why, given such an immoral role model, Cesare took it as the norm to take a woman to his bed and throw her out of it when he got tired of her.

Poor Jilly!

Glancing up at him, Milly noted with a peculiar twisting sensation in her tummy that the slight breeze from the sea had ruffled his short, dark as night hair. It made him look more approachable, less the hard-nosed, ultra sophisticated business tycoon, and it was again impressed on her exactly why her up-until-now inconstant sister had at last fallen truly, deeply in love. Very few women would be able to resist his potent brand of sexual charisma.

'Almost there.'

The effect of his voice rippled through her like a mild electric shock. Smooth as silk, consoling? Her heart pattering she narrowed her eyes against the sun. They had crested the brow of the hill and a shallow wooded valley lay before them. On the opposite side, its back to the hill, beyond which she could glimpse the sea and the sand of a small cove, was a sturdy stone house facing the green valley. A quiet, secluded place, ideal for lovers.

'Why have you brought me here?' She didn't want to know the answer because she knew she wouldn't like it but she had to ask because not knowing was getting to her. And his reply made her feel giddy.

'Why do you think, Jilly?'

The slanting smile on his shamelessly sexy mouth and the glinting, terrifyingly intimate light in those stunning eyes made her tummy loop over, forcing her to recall why this secluded hideaway on an uninhabited island had been built by his womanising father. Had he given her that snippet of information to make sure she made the connection?

He and Jilly had been lovers. Did he mean to take up where they'd left off? Demand her presence in his bed—away from his grandmother's sharp eyes and knowing smiles—in part payment for the massive debt she had accumulated by, according to his warped and cynical mind, forging those cheques?

Her heart squeezed in a severe contraction and her legs turned into wavering pillars of cotton wool. Surely he couldn't mean that! And, if he did, what on earth was she to do?

Looking down into her suddenly pale as milk face Cesare bit back a peal of husky laughter. Aside from her looks, her imposter rating would be lower than nought out of ten. She'd obviously got the message loud and clear and it had floored her. Didn't she know how her twin would have reacted to such a neatly couched invitation? Like a heat seeking missile homing in on a coveted target. All over him like a second skin.

'Come, I'll help you. The track's steep in places.'

Milly shuddered right down to her toes as he took her hand, the warmth of his soft, silky tone, the heat of his skin as his strong lean fingers closed around hers made her heart beat in a frenzy, her lungs struggling painfully because, try as she might, she couldn't seem to breathe.

Yet, uncaring breaker of hearts as she guessed him to be, he was more than careful as he helped her to negotiate the trickier places, only releasing her hand as they came to the paved area in front of the house.

Windows lay open and the stout wooden door was unlocked; obviously he had no fear of squatters or thieves intent on lifting anything they could carry away.

Mild surprise deepened to bewilderment as he ushered her into a square stone-flagged room that appeared to double as kitchen and informal living area.

Flowers in a terra-cotta bowl graced the central chunky pine table and near a small but functional looking cooker a fridge hummed gently.

Driven by feminine curiosity, Milly dived to open the fridge door and survey the lavish contents. She turned, her eyes wide. 'If no one else lives here, how did this stuff get here?' Had he lied? Were there other people on this island, someone she could turn to for help if he left her here after discovering—as he surely would eventually—that she wasn't who she claimed to be?

'By motor launch, not by magic.' His slight smile registered superior amusement. 'I have a caretaker on the mainland who, apart from checking up on the property from time to time, sees it is stocked if I phone him to tell him I'm going to be here. He gets the generator working, makes sure the water pump is functioning properly and soon.' One strongly marked brow elevated mockingly. 'Did you imagine I brought you here to starve or exist on fish from the sea? If so, you'd have had to do the catching of them. I do not own such patience.'

Face flaming, her chin notched up by several degrees, Milly faced the unwelcome truth that they were indeed alone here.

She ought to have known how the other half lived. Just one word and a minion would be found to carry out orders at a moment's notice! Silly of her to have overlooked that fact of a life!

And she wasn't about to ask again exactly why he had brought her here and risk another loaded answer. Instead she said tightly, 'Show me where I'm supposed to sleep and tell me what you want for lunch. I'm sure you expect me to wait on you!'

Because he wouldn't know how to boil water.

He might be a whiz at doing whatever clever stuff he did to earn a dazzling living, but brought up surrounded by a platoon of servants, anxious to cater to his slightest wish, he wouldn't have a domesticated bone in his body.

'Now there's a thought!' Slumbrous eyes scorched her, and Milly hastily looked away. He was lethally attractive and she sure as Hades wasn't going to follow her twin down that fatal track. She heaved a sigh of relief when he picked up her suitcase and led her up the staircase tucked away at the far side of the room.

There were two doors leading off the square landing. The first he flung open revealed a bathroom of almost clinical utility, the second a bedroom that contained the biggest bed she had ever laid eyes on and not much else.

Did Cesare, following his father's track record, bring his women here? Had he brought Jilly? If so, she had goofed badly when she'd queried the lavish supply of foodstuffs, asked where she would sleep, because there appeared to be only this one bedroom.

So where would he sleep? Her throat closed and her stomach churned with the weirdest sensation she had ever experienced. Whipping round on her sandalled feet, intent on telling him that there was no way she was sharing a bed with him and if he had brought her here with that in mind he was going to have to think again.

But there was just empty space where he had been and from downstairs she could hear his tuneful whistle. She ground her teeth in frustration. He sounded in a good mood, was her ireful thought.

Looking forward to making the woman he'd dragged back to Italy to make reparation for her supposed sins, pay off part of her dues in his bed?

CHAPTER SIX

MILLY HAD STRETCHED her wash and brush up into the best part of an hour she realised guiltily when she finally glanced at her watch. Most of that time had been spent leaning out of the bedroom window, breathing the warm scented air and making herself concentrate on nothing else but the view of the shallow wooded valley, the arc of the blue sky overhead, soaking up the utter tranquility. Anything to take her mind off her decidedly dodgy situation.

In any other circumstances she would have loved being here, especially with the man she loved. It was the perfect place for a romantic idyll.

And where that had come from she had no

idea. The wayward thought shocked her. She didn't have a man to love, here or anywhere else!

Unlike her sister, to whom the male of the species gravitated like moths to a brilliant light, Milly hadn't had much to do with the opposite sex. Quiet and unsure of herself, always deep in her twin's shadow, she hadn't exactly been sought after and had certainly never been in love.

Her first date had been a disaster. Sixteen years old and, compared with Jilly, still wet behind the ears, she'd been hugely flattered when, out of the blue, the local pin-up, Mitch Farraday, had asked her out.

He'd been earthily good-looking, full of himself, pushy. Her girl friends had all drooled over him. But the date had ended up in a scary tussle at the back of the cinema with him calling her vile names. He had taken it for granted that buying her a seat in the stalls fully entitled him to have sex. It had horrified her and she'd fought him off like a wild spitting cat.

It had frightened her, had put her off the male sex for ages. Then she'd met Bruce. Twelve years her senior, an accountant, he'd lived with his widowed mother.

He'd called into the shop to buy a pot plant and they'd got talking. Discovering a mutual interest in visiting local gardens open to the public, he'd returned a week later and invited her to accompany him and his mother to Bassett Hall gardens, an annual pilgrimage for them, apparently. And because she'd heard of the acres of rhododendrons and azaleas—at their best at that time of the year, the lakes and grottos, she'd accepted. Without her own transport she hadn't been able to get there under her own steam.

And because Bruce was solid and worthy, without a flash bone in his body, and she was comfortable in his company they had seen each other once a week for the last two years.

He was a pleasant companion. He made no sexual demands. It had only been after the death of her mother that things had changed, subtle hints from him and not so subtle ones from his mother about settling down, formalising their relationship.

Sighing, Milly turned away from the window. She liked Bruce—and his mother—but she didn't love him and never would. She'd been trying to think of a way to tell him, before he decided to come out with a proposal. She didn't want to hurt his feelings or his pride.

But Cesare had happened. His misconceptions about her twin, his threats.

In the turmoil she hadn't given poor Bruce a thought. He'd be worried about her and she felt really bad about that. But there was nothing she could do about it until she got back to the mainland. She could phone him and tell him she'd taken a temporary job as a companion. And thinking about Bruce—something she rarely did unless she was actually with him—was, she recognised, a cowardly delaying tactic.

Sooner or later she was going to have to

face Cesare, carry on the deception as best she could and hope to discover why exactly he had brought her here. And hope to heaven that it wasn't what she thought it was!

Sex.

She was pretty sure Jilly had confidently expected marriage. Was as sure as she could be that her twin had taken off, hurting and humiliated, the moment that brute had told her that all he wanted from her was hot sex.

Now he believed he had a hold over his grandmother's companion. That with his threat to go to the law hanging over her she'd do exactly as he wished. So did he think he could take up where he'd left off? Did the idea of that brand of dominating sexual revenge give him a buzz?

According to his warped mind, Jilly had stolen an as yet unspecified amount of money. Was he now intent on exacting repayment? As Jilly's stand-in the thought was enough to give her nightmares!

Her tummy muscles tight with nerves, Milly

straightened her spine until it was ramrod stiff and made her way downstairs to set about making lunch. Not that she was hungry, but he, conscienceless, would be. And it would give her something to do, maybe even take her mind off the mess she was in for all of two seconds.

To be met by the sight of Cesare confidently dividing the contents of a pan between two plates with the panache of a professional.

'I was just about to call you.' A warm smile, lacking guile, then a slight inclination of his far-too-handsome head. 'I thought we'd eat outside. The wine's uncorked; perhaps you'd like to pour it.'

He'd found a small table and two chairs from somewhere, she noted, as she stepped out on to the sun-soaked paved area in front of the cottage. The edges of the white table-cloth moved lazily in the gentle breeze.

Cutlery, glasses, a basket of bread rolls and a slab of creamy butter on a blue earthenware plate. Her hands shook as she poured a little red wine into both glasses and she sank on to one of the chairs because her knees gave way as he appeared.

'Tell me what you think.' Cesare slid a plate in front of her and retreated to the chair on the other side of the table. 'When I cook I like to experiment.' An eyebrow quirked in rare self-disparagement. 'Sometimes it goes horribly wrong!'

Against all her expectations the delicate aroma enticed the appetite she thought she'd lost for ever and, struggling with confusion, Milly forked up lemony rice and one of the perfectly cooked succulent prawns. The dish was garnished with mushrooms and roasted peppers and was absolutely delicious.

Suddenly ravenous, she reached for a roll and lavished it with butter and Cesare demanded softly, 'Well, what's the verdict?'

'Fabulous—you can cook for me any time you like!' Her first real smile for days lit up her features and he returned it with a devastating grin of his own before starting on his meal.

He could actually seem human, Milly marvelled, trying to see through the mists of confusion that were now fogging her brain. And how easily, naturally, she could respond to him was an eye-opener! A tiny frown furrowed her brow. She'd honestly believed that Cesare Saracino wouldn't know how to boil a kettle and was too arrogant to even want to know how to perform that most mundane of tasks. Yet he'd set to and produced one of the most delicious meals she'd ever eaten.

She'd been proved wrong about that; was she also wrong about believing him to be all bad? And another thought struck her a savage blow. Had she been acting like a brain dead gnat when she'd entered this utterly distasteful deception?

She was trapped here. Once back on the mainland she would be trapped at the villa. With blithe stupidity she'd seen herself tracking Jilly down before Cesare reached her, combing the streets of Florence, calling the contact number her twin had given when she'd worked there, questioning her friends and her former employer in the hope of gaining a clue to her present whereabouts.

Fat chance! She might just as well decide to explore the dark side of the moon. Jumping on a bus or taking a taxi into Florence wasn't an option when she had no money and, as Cesare had stringently pointed out, she wouldn't be earning any either!

Reflectively she sipped her wine and Cesare, leaning back against his chair, one arm hooked casually over the back, said softly, 'A penny for them.'

'You'd be wasting your money!' Milly came back abstractedly, fighting uncertainty over what to do.

Carry on in her role as her sister or come clean and confess all, throw herself on his mercy. After all, he thought she was, in his entrenched opinion, the devious Jilly and he'd been nothing but kind and friendly since they'd reached the island. A prelude to getting her to share that huge bed with him? Should she rid herself of this hare-brained deception once and for all?

It was what her conscience told her she wanted but she'd jumped in without thinking back in England, she wouldn't do it again. She'd have to think it out properly.

'I wonder. I'm fairly canny when it comes to handing out such vast sums of money!'

Milly's breath caught in her throat. He looked so relaxed, so spectacularly good to look at; the hand that toyed with the stem of his wineglass was strong yet achingly elegant. Beautiful hands to match the rest of his perfect male physique. And that slight smile, tilted at one corner—the slumbrously wicked gleam in those dark, darkly seductive, eyes as they locked with hers, was more than she could take. Her breath was quickening and, to her deep shame, she could feel her nipples pressing against the silky top, tight, over-sensitive buds.

He was lethal! Jilly would have been a

pushover. And in all honesty Milly couldn't blame her!

Unable to prolong what suddenly and shatteringly seemed like a not so subtle form of torture—frantic heartbeat, trembling lower limbs, her skin scorchingly hot—Milly shot to her feet and got out through a throat that had gone suffocatingly tight, 'I'll do the dishes.'

'Leave them.' His voice was lazy but there was nothing lazy about the inescapable grip of those long beautiful fingers as they closed around her wrist. He rose to his feet, still holding her wrist, and her face flooded with hot pink as his darkly veiled eyes drifted over her body with a blatant lack of inhibition.

He couldn't make his expectations more explicit, she thought wildly, out and out panic warring with the most unnerving sensation of being on a perpetual roller coaster ride.

The strong, imperative physical awareness was something she wasn't equipped to handle. She most definitely didn't need it.

What type of creature was she to be turned on by a monster, just because he was the most handsome, sexy and wickedly charismatic male she was ever likely to set her eyes on?

And when he stepped round the table, released her wrist, gave her a tap on her curvy backside that lingered that little bit too long and said in a voice like melted chocolate, 'Put on a pair of walking shoes; I'll introduce you to my island,' Milly fled, her haste making her heartbeat race even faster.

As Cesare cleared the decks and made short work of washing the dishes and returning the kitchen to pristine order a small satisfied smile hovered at the corners of his long mouth.

The imposter was running scared! A job well done. His off-the-wall decision to bring her here was completely justified. And he couldn't believe that she could be so naive. She still believed she was successfully deceiving him.

Santo cielo! How could she be so naive? A deliberately steamy look and she coloured like the sunrise, trembled. Didn't she know how her twin would have reacted?

The Jilly Lee he knew would have returned that look with interest, parted her glossy lips and lowered her artificially enhanced lashes over sultry green come-bed-me eyes. She would have smouldered, not trembled like a sacrificial virgin!

The imposter, Milly, gave herself away at practically every turn and he was debating how much longer he would wait before he dropped his bombshell when she appeared at the head of the stairs.

She was still wearing the blue top that skimmed her pert and perfect breasts, and the cropped white jeans that clung to her slender, beautifully formed thighs. And on her feet she wore what he supposed she classed as walking shoes. Flat soles and thin straps, gladiator-style.

But the thing that riveted his attention, squeezed his heart, was the way that stress had darkened her clear green eyes, widening them with a mute appeal that pierced him like an arrow, the way her soft unpainted lips hovered between a tremble and a wary smile.

Out of nowhere came the unwelcome feeling that he was behaving badly, married to an intense desire to care for her, protect her, keep her safe, kiss that lovely, vulnerable mouth until it melted into passion until desire and wanting replaced the stress in those beautiful stress filled eyes.

She was descending the stairs now. Slowly, uncertainly. Cesare closed his eyes briefly to shut her out and cursed himself for reacting like a green fool, an immature sucker for an exquisitely feminine face and form.

The vulnerable, little girl lost look had to be an act; he had to remember that or he'd find himself believing he was behaving like a monster! That he was wrong.

He was never wrong!

Like her twin, she would have left innocence and purity behind her soon after she'd first climbed out of the cradle! Despite her perfect, unsullied beauty—the opposite of her twin's brash in-your-face would-be sexiness—she was just as devious and deceitful as her freeloading, thieving sister, he reminded himself with brutal firmness.

And later this evening—let her stew a little longer, not knowing what he expected of her in her role as Jilly—he would tell her what he knew and shock her into telling him where her twin was.

She would know; of course she would. Back in England she hadn't corrected his initial belief that she was the absconding Jilly, as she surely would have done had she had an honest bone in her body!

As soon as he'd left she would have contacted her sister—who might even have been skulking in the flat above for all he knew. They would have concocted the plan between them. As long as Milly could keep up the deception Jilly would be free to disappear again, cover her tracks completely. And as soon as she thought her sister was safe from his demands for retribution Milly too would slope away in the night.

As she drew level he forced a light tone, a smile. 'Let's go.' And turned away before she could sense the anger building inside him.

'Wait.' Firmly said but inside she was a quaking wreck. At some moment during the time she'd spent searching through her caseful of Jilly's cast offs for something remotely resembling walking shoes it had hit her that she couldn't go on with this. With every moment that passed the deception became more distasteful. Intrinsically honest, she hated living a lie and, to be brutally truthful, she wasn't brave enough to face his formidable anger when she gave herself away—as she surely would. Better to confess first. That way she could show herself to be not all bad in his eyes. Though why his opinion of her should matter one way or the other she brushed aside as being unimportant.

True, so far he hadn't had any suspicions that anything was wrong, that she wasn't who she was pretending to be. He'd actually been rather nice, flirtatious at one unforgettable point. Intent on getting Jilly back in his bed even though the No Marriage proviso was still writ large? After all, as he saw it, Jilly was in no position to refuse his demands.

The whole business was making her feel thoroughly ashamed of herself, not to mention horribly nervous on her own account, but now, against her former reasoning she'd reached the snap conclusion that she had to carry on with it. Opening her mouth, telling him to wait prior to making her confession, she'd had a sudden blinding mental flashback to the way her twin had always been so protective of her when they were growing up. She couldn't let her down now. Somehow she was going to have to find a way to track Jilly down before he did.

The broad shoulders beneath the soft white cotton stiffened perceptibly and after a strained moment he slowly turned. The smile he gave her was breathtaking, one ebony brow was raised slightly, half questioning, half humorous, adding even more charisma to those lean hard features. 'You want to borrow some footwear that won't disintegrate after the first dozen yards?'

'No.' If only it were that simple! If she were to carry on with this ridiculous deception, then for her own sake she had to get things straight—never mind how Jilly would have reacted in this situation. Slim shoulders tense, her soft mouth firm, she levelled at him, 'I want to know why you thought it necessary to bring me here.' A deep breath. 'And where you'll be sleeping tonight.'

CHAPTER SEVEN

'YOU KNOW WHY I brought you here,' Cesare responded lightly and with the apparent sincerity that hid the initial much darker intent. 'As I said to Nonna—in your hearing, as I remember—after your recent loss you need a break. I am not a complete monster.'

As her lovely eyes darkened with pain at the reminder of her mother's death Cesare fisted his hands and cursed himself, bitterly regretting the glib distortion of his motives.

A devious little liar she might be, but she was capable of having deep feelings.

Unlike her twin.

The hedonistic Jilly would have shed a few facile tears at the loss of a parent, he assessed. But, knowing her as he did, he couldn't imagine her having a single unselfish emotion. When pressed about her family she'd dismissed them with that irritating tinkling laugh, claiming her mother to be small-town, small-minded and her kid sister as being practical and deadly dull, too boring—Not our kind of people, not worth talking about, dahling.

But this one—Ebony brows clenched, he narrowed his eyes on her expressive features. Silky lashes were lowered to veil her dark green eyes, her soft pink mouth trembled just slightly and her glorious breasts were heaving with suppressed emotion. Yes, this twin had deep feelings, despite her manifest faults—

'Come.' His voice soft with sympathy and regret for his own insensitivity, he slotted an arm around her shoulders, drawing her into the sunlight. 'We will walk, relax.' Unbidden, his long fingers caressed the firm warm flesh of her upper arm before he realised what he was doing.

When he did he suffered the sharp reminder of her duplicity and his arm dropped back to his side in double quick time. His voice was flat with cynicism as he made himself focus on her deception and the punishment he was meting out. 'As for the sleeping arrangements, there is a ground floor bedroom beyond the kitchen. If that is a disappointment to you, you only have to say so. On the other hand—' his voice purred now, surprising him by its husky quality '—you might find yourself sleepless, wondering when I will give in to my baser instincts and seek the pleasures of your bed.'

'More pasta?' His voice was slow, deep and nerve-quiveringly sexy.

Milly shook her head, trying to cope with the sudden, highly unwelcome way her tummy muscles went into hot spasm. Nothing to do with the spicy tomato sauce and spaghetti they'd cooked together, working companionably enough with just the odd tingling *frisson* when they'd touched, hands brushing or bare arm gliding against bare arm, and everything to do with the way he made her feel.

As if she were walking a tightrope in a high wind without a safety net.

He'd been lying when he'd said he'd brought her here to give her a break; did he think she was stupid enough to believe that? He thought she was Jilly, his ex-lover, the woman he was blisteringly angry with. This so-called break was a punishment. And the worst thing was she had no idea what form that punishment would take.

And on another level entirely, she felt utterly disorientated. Nothing made sense.

Why had she warmed to him during the long afternoon as he'd shown her around his island, forgetting why she was here, the depth of her own deceit?

Why had she relaxed enough to enjoy every single moment of it?

Why couldn't she blank out that refusing-to-budge memory of exactly how she'd felt when those long tanned fingers had caressed her arm, or the way he'd slipped a protective arm around her waist as they'd stood on top of the cliffs above the cove nearest the cottage, looking down to the white sands far below. 'Tomorrow we will bathe,' he'd told her, 'take a picnic, spend the day.'

She'd felt dizzy. Not because the narrow zigzagging track down to the secluded beach looked hair-raising but because the warmth of his strong hand clamped to her waist had sent a quiver of heat across her breasts, rippling and stinging there until it had arrowed down to the pit of her stomach with devastating accuracy, making her go weak at the knees and catch her breath.

Now he said, 'You are tired? You would like to go to bed?'

His low, husky drawl made it sound like an invitation. A slow burn ignited her skin. If it had really been an invitation would she have had the strength of will to turn it down? Or would she, like her poor betrayed sister, have accepted it with open arms, giving him her love only to have it tossed aside?

But it had been nothing of the sort, she

decided shortly. What had he said earlier?
That she would spend a sleepless night wondering if he would give in to his baser instincts and seek her bed.

Meaning he would have to overcome his
fastidious distaste for having sex with a
woman he believed to be a thief! But he'd
been her sister's lover before. Was he still in
lust with her?

Lying sleepless—nerves screaming—and
wondering!

No, thank you!

'I'm fine,' she said, glossing over her raging
internal turmoil. 'I'll sit awhile. It's so peace-
ful.'

And it was. Despite his presence.

Darkness was closing in. They'd eaten
supper outside. There was a candle in a glass
bowl on the table and she could hear the
mesmeric whisper of the incoming tide. If it
weren't for worrying about his intentions, ag-
onising over the way she was drawn to him,
she could have believed she was in Paradise.

'Fine!' Cesare scoffed silently. She was nothing of the sort. Tension came off her in almost tangible waves. Worrying about the prospect of his probable sexual demands? As he'd intended her to, he conceded toughly. A small, easily justified revenge for the way she had set out to deceive him.

A contrary impulse to rise, go to her, massage the taut muscles of her neck and shoulders until she relaxed, leant back into him while he gave in to temptation and slid his hands down to slip beneath the top that left little to the imagination to caress her inviting breasts was slapped down hard before the erotic wanderings of his imagination could do any real damage.

Initially he'd fully intended to hit her with what he knew this evening, demand she tell him the whereabouts of the twin she was impersonating so badly. But during the day something had changed. He didn't know how or why or even what, but changed it had.

He needed more time to find out what she

was really like. He grimaced. More time to analyse his own ambivalent reactions to her was probably nearer the truth.

As he settled back into the shadows his long mouth curved with hastily manufactured cynicism as he watched her reach for the wineglass he'd refilled. Her hand shook. She set the glass down again. Fearful of spilling the contents, betraying herself?

He'd have to be brain dead to have missed the signs. The way her soft flesh had quivered whenever he'd touched her, the tell-tale huff of indrawn breath, the unmistakable peaking of her tight nipples against her silky top.

So would she welcome him if he went to her bed? The unbidden thought had shattering appeal, set his skin tingling with the slow burn of desire.

Dio mio! His tough jaw-line hard, Cesare shot to his feet. Male lust was taking him places he didn't want to be. The object of this exercise had been to punish her, not himself!

'Finish your wine.' His voice emerged

coldly. He didn't look at her, didn't trust himself to see the look of soft vulnerability she seemed incapable of hiding and not do something about it. Something he'd bitterly regret. 'I'll see you in the morning.'

As Cesare swept back into the cottage Milly expelled a breath she hadn't realised she'd been holding. She heard an inner door slam. The door to the ground floor sleeping quarters he'd talked about?

Whatever. He was suddenly riven with anger, that much she did know. But didn't know why.

She passed a hand over her forehead in an attempt to rub away the tense frown lines. He was angry with Jilly, not with her, she had to remind herself. Keeping up with her dual identity was really getting to her.

She was finding the deception more than distasteful but at least it bought time she consoled herself as she hauled herself to her feet and began to stack the used dishes. More time for her to somehow figure a way of tracking her twin down, more time for Jilly to get over her going-nowhere affair with the charismatic far-too-sexy Italian tycoon so that she'd be in a stronger emotional state to argue her case, convince him that there had been some dreadful mistake.

And more time for her unwilling fascination with him to develop into a deeper phase? was the utterly disquieting thought that popped into her head.

Thrusting it aside as brutally as she knew how, she carried the dishes through and washed them at the deep stone sink and, drying her hands, listened to the silence until she felt calmer.

A door on the far wall, tucked between the dresser and a painted closet, a door she hadn't noticed before, must lead to the bedroom he was using. Annoyingly, her eyes would keep straying to it. As if she were expecting Cesare to emerge, black hair damp from the shower, droplets glistening on the golden skin of his perfectly crafted torso, a towel slung low on his narrow hips?

Expecting? Wanting?

Ashamed of the burning heat, the sullen ache, that was claiming the most private part of her anatomy, she dragged in a shaky breath, turning her back on the door and carefully folded the towel she'd been using, naming herself for the worst kind of fool.

At least his manner of leaving her—anger because of what he thought Jilly had done taking precedence over what she, the imposter, guessed was his callous decision to exact sexual part payment for her perceived wrongdoing meant that she'd be safe from his desire to carry on from where he and her twin had left off.

Safe, too, from her own emerging weakness?

Even so, if there had been a key to her bedroom door she would have locked it.

'The sea is waiting. Remember?'

The soft drawl brought Milly out of her troubled sleep at the speed of light, as if every nerve in her body had been hit by a bolt of lightning. Jerking up against the pillows, she belatedly tugged the sheet up to cover her breasts, bitterly regretting her decision to slip naked between the cool crisp sheets after her shower last night.

Embarrassment colouring her cheeks, deep emerald eyes flinchingly sought him beneath the tousled pale silk of her fringe. Sought and locked.

Casually leaning against the doorframe, incredibly sexy in narrow-fitting jeans and a sleeveless olive green T-shirt, he looked magnificent, magnetic, all male strength, lean lines, hard muscles.

Her breath stopped in her throat. Her eyes slid up to his face. That slight utterly devastating smile, the straight Roman nose that flared a little when he was angry, the dark as night eyes veiled now by impossibly thick and silky lashes.

It was so unfair!

If her worldly-wise sophisticated twin, who'd been wrapping besotted males around her little finger ever since she'd reached her late teens, hadn't been able to resist falling for him then how the hell was she supposed to cope?

Conquests had always come so easily to Jilly, and had just as easily bored her. She'd always walked away without a single regret. But this time, if her hunch was right, Jilly had met more than her match. She'd finally fallen in love and Milly couldn't blame her.

Worriedly she recalled that last postcard from Florence. It must have been sent just before Jilly had joined the Saracino household. She had been so sure that in the future money would be no object, that she would be able to repay her debts. She must have been convinced that her new lover would soon be her husband.

'Get ready. We'll eat breakfast on the beach and swim later,' he delivered, fascinated by the blush that bloomed like wild roses on her cheeks. And turned away before he could get too fascinated by her naked state beneath the tangled sheet, tangled in a way that left one

long, smooth and shapely leg exposed all the
way to the apex of a creamy thigh, sternly reminding himself of the questions he had lined
up for the lying little witch today.

He turned away, leaving the room, and
Milly released a pent-up sigh of deep relief.
She couldn't believe how vulnerable she'd
felt, lying here in a sheet and nothing else.

And the way he'd been looking at her, as if
he could see right through the fine white
cotton! Her whole body blushed and, to take
her mind off it, she leapt out of bed and told
herself she was doing fine. Just fine.

As she rummaged through her suitcase for
something to wear she mentally ticked off
all the pros.

So far he still had no idea that she wasn't Jilly.
While that state of affairs remained he
wasn't out there hunting down the real Jilly,
no doubt with a pair of handcuffs in his
pocket.

He hadn't made any attempt to get up close
and personal.

She was sensible enough to slap him down if he did. Wasn't she?

As for the cons.

There was the rest of the week to get through.

But she could hack it!

Sifting through Jilly's cast-offs, she extracted an outrageous black bikini. Three triangles of fabric and a sort of thong thing. Her face went scarlet. Cleo must have added it to the pile while she had been helping her decide what to take. She, Milly, would never dream of flaunting herself in something so revealing!

She thrust it back into the case, then sat back on her heels, forcing herself to face facts.

Jilly would have no hesitation in wearing the thing. She was supposed to be Jilly, wasn't she? So, to keep the impersonation going and not get found out, she was going to have to behave and dress as her twin would.

Not giving herself time to think about it,

she put it on and smartly covered up with a pair of very brief pale lemon coloured shorts, the weird sandals and a sleeveless blouse in a toning, slightly darker lemon that tied just below her breasts, leaving her midriff bare, and went down to the kitchen before she could chicken out.

'Coffee.' Cesare pushed a mug of the fragrant brew across the kitchen table. He was seated, long legs outstretched, encased in faded denim. He was naked to the waist now; the tanned skin that stretched over whipcord muscles gleamed with health and vigour. Milly's throat jerked. He was too much!

Feeling hot and bothered beneath his lazy scrutiny, she took the mug and carried it to the open door and leaned against the frame, looking out over the lush green valley so she didn't have to look at him, doing her damnedest to appear relaxed. If only she knew what sort of game he was playing! It seemed as though he was making up the rules as he went along!

Before they'd arrived on the island he'd treated her as if she were beneath contempt, dark eyes filled with cold scorn, reinforcing what she already knew. That he was only suffering her presence beneath his roof and not hauling her before a judge because his grandmother had taken a real liking to her lively young companion. And his beloved Nonna's happiness and wellbeing counted more than his own satisfaction at seeing her face prosecution.

Yet now—

'It is a beautiful day, yes?'

Milly hadn't heard him come to stand behind her and the sheer sensuality of his voice made her breath lock in her lungs and sent a skitter of sensation down the length of her spine.

She moved away, putting her coffee mug down on the outdoor table and managed, 'So it is,' and wondered when his motives would become clear. And what they were.

Getting her—Jilly—back into his bed? From the rapid alteration in his attitude, it kind of looked that way. The unwanted conclusion took her breath away and she snatched a deep gulp of fresh air, breathing in the scent of the sea and the abundant wild herbs.

'Shall we go?' He had joined her, a backpack hooked over one shoulder, bare feet in canvas deck shoes, sunlight gleaming on the skin of his torso making it look like oiled silk.

Her legs decidedly shaky, Milly followed, keeping behind him as the track leading to the cliff top narrowed. The way down to the beach looked more hair-raising than it had done yesterday.

'Take my hand.'

'I can manage.'

No way did Milly want physical contact. But he ignored her, taking her delicate hand in his much stronger one and he couldn't have taken more care of her as he helped her negotiate the scary path if she'd been his best beloved. And observation that for a silly moment made her wish that she really was.

Her face red with embarrassment at the way her thoughts were taking her, Milly tugged her hand free the moment they reached the soft white sand of the cove, wishing again she'd never embarked on this crazy scheme. She had to remind herself firmly that now that she had to carry on with it as she watched him drop the rucksack in the shade of a rock.

Then he turned to face the sea, his dark head thrown back, his perfectly proportioned body stretching with sensual animal grace as he welcomed the warmth of the sun on his bronzed skin.

Milly told herself to look away but she couldn't. He was magnificent, and when he turned to her, a grin making him look irresistible, and said, 'We'll swim first. Race you to the water!' a skitter of something wicked attacked the length of her spine.

Those long tanned fingers of his were at his belt buckle. Milly's heart began a wild tattoo as she became cringingly aware of the scanty nature of the so-called swim wear beneath her shorts and top.

She could always decline, refuse to go anywhere near the water. There was no law that said she had to.

But Jilly would never pass up on such an opportunity to flaunt her assets in front of such an eminently desirable male. She was no shrinking violet! Milly knew her twin inside out, knew how she would behave.

Here in this magical place, alone with the man she loved, she would be hoping to lure him into changing his mind about the veto on marriage, tempt him and then protest her innocence in the matter of theft. Milly was sure she couldn't go that far, it was too dangerous. The protestations of innocence would have to come from her twin—and the tempting bit. But if she was going to continue to act the part of her twin then at least she had to stay in character.

As she forced herself to untie her top she noted that Cesare had shed his jeans and was now clad in brief black swim trunks that did zero to disguise his manhood. Gulping, she turned her back on him, her heart fluttering, nervous tension threatening to pull her apart as she reluctantly shed her top and muttered, 'You go ahead. I don't do racing.'

Cesare didn't move. She was clearly uncomfortable. Desperately uncomfortable. Her back, naked save the narrow ribbons that must hold her bikini top in place, was taut with inner tension. Her fingers hesitated at the waistband of the shorts she was wearing.

Compassion twisted deep in his chest. Had her hard-nosed twin forced her into this charade against her will? It was beginning to look like it. The Jilly Lees of this world went full tilt to get what they wanted, never mind who got hurt in the process.

His hands fisted then uncurled at his sides as she took the plunge and stepped out of her shorts revealing smooth firm buttocks, long shapely legs. She was so beautiful. His heart jerked. And then she half turned and his mouth ran dry. The three scraps of fabric that pretended to be a bikini were outrageous, the bottom half barely held in place by a thong.

Exactly the sort of siren stuff her twin would choose. Plainly not expecting him to be still waiting, she shot him a wild look, her skin flaming, then fled for the sea. Following more slowly, Cesare actively disliked himself for putting her through this.

He should have told her he knew what was going on the moment they had set foot on the island, demanded to know where her twin was. Not played games.

Apart from short hair, short fingernails, she and Jilly were physically identical. Yet he had never been remotely attracted to her twin, finding her overt sexiness a distinct turn-off. Which led him to the uncomfortable conclusion that he was definitely attracted to the softer, gentler version.

Against his will. But still attracted.

As the cool aquamarine waters closed around her overheated body Milly relaxed just a little.

She had truly believed he would have already been in the sea. But he'd been standing there all the time, watching her with those dark unreadable sexy eyes while she'd stripped off her top clothes. From the back she would have looked naked, she thought with a shudder of deep embarrassment, and from the front not a whole lot better. The tiny scraps of fabric did more to tantalise than to conceal.

And the way he'd looked at her—well, she wasn't going to think about that! Striking out in a racing crawl, she kicked out for the headland that sheltered the cove.

She was a strong swimmer and loved the water. In fact she had won cups during her schooldays. It was the one area where she had left Jilly far behind. Jilly hated physical exertion.

For the first time since she'd made the momentous decision to go along with his belief that she was her twin sister, Milly felt free, at ease with herself and the watery elements as she stroked through the swells.

But the rocky headland looked no nearer and at this rate she wouldn't reach it until a week on Sunday—

A sudden surge, the impression that she was being attacked by an extra large and determined octopus, had Milly gasping, squirming as Cesare's head emerged, sea water running in rivulets from his sleek head, his arms tight around her body.

'What do you think you're doing?' she spluttered in outrage. She had headed out here to escape him for a short but precious time. But he'd followed. Wasn't the ocean large enough for both of them?

He was spoiling her pleasure, wiping out that glorious feeling of freedom. 'Let go of me!' He was stopping her progress, what there had been of it. And worse, far worse, his grip meant their bodies were touching, breast to thigh. She could feel the hard determined strength of him against her slender curves and it was just too much. Her heart was pounding with the effort to stop herself from pressing much, much closer, winding arms and legs around every bit of him she could reach.

'Saving you from drowning.' His mouth was taut. The current here is deadly. As I would have warned you if you'd hung around long enough to listen.' Treading water, he shook his head with a snap of impatience, water droplets scattering. 'Head back. Now!'

Shuddering, Milly became aware of the undertow she'd unknowingly been fighting for the last few minutes, dragging them steadily and inexorably towards the horizon.

Frightened now, she struck out, fighting against the current, heading back to the distant shoreline, aware that Cesare was shadowing her, modifying his progress to hers, and she was more grateful than he would ever know because, strangely, she felt that nothing could harm her while he was with her.

When at last they were clear of the undertow he powered ahead of her and, seconds later, it seemed, he stood up, finding bottom, the gently swelling water reaching his trim waist.

Waiting. His features like a thunderstorm.

Milly swam slowly towards him, her lungs still burning from her strenuous fight against the undertow, the calm surface water hiding the danger. As soon as she was within reach Cesare slid his hands beneath her arms and hauled her to her feet and bit out with blistering fury, 'Don't ever pull a stunt like that again!' his eyes black with fury. His hands tightened on her slender shoulders. *'Dio mio! You could have died, you bird-brained little fool!'*

And he could have died trying to save her, was her initial mortifying thought, fully aware that he would not have stood idly by and watched her put herself in danger. But his bellowed insult moved her to self defence and she raised her chin, her heart still pounding from her efforts, her breasts heaving, pushing against the clinging, useless scraps of fabric and snapped right back, 'How was I to know? And you can stop yelling!'

She shimmied her shoulders wildly, trying

to loosen his punishing grip, but his hands just slid down to her waist, tugging her towards him with a bitten out, 'You—' Then his mouth was on hers with forceful, angry passion, one hand pressing her body into his until she could feel the imprint of every muscle, the shocking hardness of his arousal against the wet quivering flesh of her tummy, the other hand behind her head, holding her against any hope of escape.

Not that escape entered her mind. She had never experienced anything like this—this hot searing passion, this crazy escalation of sensation, setting every atom of her flesh on fire.

Milly's arms wound up to coil around his neck, her lips parting in instinctive eager welcome and she heard him groan, low and deep, his mouth gentling, moving sensually as his tongue stroked hers for giddying moments before moving down and taking the hard crest of her breast after nudging the unresisting scrap of wet fabric aside.

Cesare moved slowly towards the shore,

taking her with him, bodies moving as one, clinging, lost in drugged pleasure, and his mouth explored now, gentle, awestruck by the sweet perfection of her, the soft hollow at her temples, the tender underside of her jaw, her throat where a pulse was beating madly. His hands moved, disposing of the flimsy scraps that were an insult to the pert glory of her peaking breasts.

Bewitching.

He was bewitched.

His hands moved, shaped her breasts then the tips of his fingers explored her tight nipples and the air in his lungs felt hot and heavy as she threw her head back, her eyes closing, her soft pink lips parted as her hips moved with instinctive rhythm against his rampant arousal.

Shock waves of sensation had him almost stumbling as his feet encountered the hot sand of the secluded beach. His mouth took hers with almost savagely passionate intent as he drew her down on to the sand and groaned with all male pleasure as she wrapped her lovely legs around his hips and trembled.

Madness.

Irresistible madness.

She was open to him. And hot. Hot. Hot.

'Bella, bella, bella—'

lovely legs around his hips and trembled...

CHAPTER EIGHT

THE DISTINCTIVE RING tone of his mobile
phone had the salutary effect of a bucket of
ice cold water. Cesare's dark head shot up.

Porca miseria. Had he run mad? He'd been
controlled by lust for the first time in his life,
forgetting who she was, who he was! It was
demeaning and he didn't like the experience.

Her hands were clinging to his shoulders.
He firmly detached them and, not looking at
her for shame, he disentangled himself,
jerked to his feet and strode over the few
paces to where he'd left his rucksack before
he'd turned insane.

Noting with deep distaste that his hands
weren't steady, he extracted the slim mobile
and ground out, *'Che?'* And went still.

Almost sobbing with a horrible mixture of shameful sexual frustration, blind panic and helpless mortification, Milly scrambled to her feet and stumbled over the soft sand and, all fingers and thumbs, began to struggle into her shorts and top.

What must he think of her? Her eyes sparkled with scalding tears and her face burned hot and scarlet. That she was an out and out slut? His for the taking!

And what was almost worse, the painful conclusion that she didn't want him to think badly of her, that his good opinion mattered— more than anything else.

How could she explain, tell him that she wasn't like that, that this sort of thing had never happened to her before—and expect him to listen, let alone believe her? And that led to another conclusion she really didn't want to have to think about.

The final irony—he thought she was Jilly, his ex-lover. He wouldn't have batted an eyelash at her frenzied response, naturally he wouldn't, cynically putting it down to a resumption of past pleasures.

It just went to show that she'd been so lost in wanting him, needing him, that she'd totally forgotten who she was supposed to be to the extent that she'd been frantically wondering how she could convince him that this sort of behaviour wasn't normal for her and what had happened had only happened because, for her, he was special.

Squirming inside with sickening embarrassment, she had to concede that she'd come within a whisker of giving herself away—in more senses than one.

If there had been no interruption their steamy encounter would have reached an inevitable conclusion. He would have known then; he wasn't stupid. She was a virgin, Jilly certainly wasn't!

Finally the top was in place, the tie ends more or less securely fastened and, her head downbent in mortification, she peered up at him through her lashes. He was speaking in his own language, his tone questioning, terse. Then he closed the phone with a snap, tossed it into the rucksack and dragged on his jeans.

The belt buckle swiftly dealt with, he scooped up the rucksack, slinging it over his shoulder, then turned to her as if he had only just recalled her existence, his brow clenched in a black frown. Milly hung her head in a vain attempt to hide the renewed flush of humiliation that burned on her face.

His voice harsh, he imparted, 'Nonna had a bad fall this morning. That was Rosa to tell me they'd just returned from Casualty. We leave for the mainland immediately.'

He was striding away and, just as he reached the cliff pathway, she caught up with him, her own troublesome problems forgotten in her anxiety for the old lady she'd liked immediately. 'Is she hurt? What happened?'

Brow clenched, he spared her a glance. 'Broken collar bone and cracked ribs. Nothing life threatening but at her age the

shock—' His voice clipped on his last word
and Milly impulsively laid a hand on his arm.

'Try not to worry,' she murmured sympa-
thetically. 'We'll soon be with her. Look,' she
suggested firmly and calmly, 'you go on
ahead, do what you need to do—rev up the
helicopter, or whatever. I'll follow, quick as I
can. And the stuff I brought with me, I'll leave
it. It's not important, so I won't need to waste
time packing.'

Cesare's eyes dropped first to the small
hand that lay consolingly on his forearm and
then lifted to her face. There was concern in
those beautiful eyes, determination writ large
on her exquisite features. His heart jerked
with something indefinable and his voice was
thick as he countered, 'You come with me. I
don't want to have to fly you to hospital
because you fell off a cliff!'

Common sense, Milly told herself as he
took her hand and helped her along every
step of the tortuous track. Of course he
wouldn't want her to miss her footing and

fall; he wouldn't want the delay of scraping her up off the rocks, she decided, determined not to read anything more into his care for her.

The way he strode rapidly ahead the moment they reached the safety of the cliff top gave credence to her assessment. He was waiting for her outside the little stone cottage when she arrived, out of breath. He had slung a casual, well worn light denim jacket over his naked torso and he enquired briefly, 'Did you mean what you said about not packing?'

'Of course. I left stuff back at the villa. I won't have to walk around naked.' And what had led her to say that she had no idea, especially when the throwaway remark earned her the glimmer of a quirky smile and a pointedly raised eyebrow before he set off across the island to the landing pad, leaving her to trot along in his wake, hot and bothered, wondering if what she felt for him was actually love. Wondering how she could be so stupid to even give that thought headroom.

* * *

The journey back to the villa was swiftly accomplished by helicopter and car, mostly in silence. Milly was aware of his impatience, the evidence of it written all over him as he braked the car to a gravel-splattering halt, slid out and strode into the villa where Rosa was waiting for him.

There was no way Milly could make head or tail of the rapid Italian conversation, but she picked out the word *dottore* and when Cesare headed for his grandmother's ground floor bedroom she followed, anxious to know how the old lady was.

The room was exactly as she remembered it from the previous time she'd come here. Tall windows opened to the warm air, gauzy curtains filtering out the harshness of the sunlight, fluttering gently in the slight breeze. The delicate tester bed with Filomena propped up against the white embroidered pillows, one arm strapped in a sling.

Cesare strode towards the old lady, lifting

the hand that wasn't confined by the sling to his lips, his voice hoarse as he murmured what Milly, hovering uncertainly in the doorway, could only suppose to be reassurances.

Then he turned to the short stout man who was packing a stethoscope into a square black bag and fired questions at him in Italian.

Feeling out of place, still in turmoil over what had taken place between her and Cesare this morning, Milly was about to turn and go to her own room when Filomena registered her presence in the doorway.

'My dear—come, sit with me!' And in the same breath, 'Cesare! English only as usual—to please me.'

Going to Filomena, Milly's legs felt unsteady and almost gave way beneath her when she saw Cesare swing round, dark colour slashing along his angular cheekbones as his glittering eyes bored into her quaking body.

Once again he had forgotten all about her and definitely didn't like being reminded that she was still on the same planet, she decided miserably, knowing that she would never be the centre of his thoughts and wishing she could be.

Trying to ignore that piece of insanity as Cesare saw the doctor out, Milly sank into the pretty pale lemon upholstered chair at the bedside and smiled with sympathy, 'Poor you—how do you feel? A bit battered?'

The old lady was pale but her eyes were smiling as she answered, 'Only when I try to move! I was careless and now I pay the price.'

'How did it happen?' Milly stroked the frail hand that lay on the white coverlet, trying to ignore the tingling sensation at the nape of her neck which told her that Cesare had returned and his black eyes were boring into the back of her head.

'Amalia and I were walking in the garden and I was so amused by her wicked gossip that I was not paying attention and missed my footing on the steps leading down to the arbour.'

'Where is the Contessa now?' Cesare had

stationed himself on the opposite side of the bed. Milly was determined not to look at him.

'She left when I was returned on a stretcher. Such a fuss! She was fearful that she would be in the way.'

'I should not have left you here with her!' Cesare pronounced on a grim note of castigation. 'If you are not even to be trusted to look where you are going!'

'Grandson, you speak as if I am a child!'

Filomena was obviously growing distressed. Milly rose to her defence. Disregarding her intention not to look at him she glared across the bed, her green eyes glinting defiantly. 'Your grandmother does not need to be grumbled at. If you can't be gentle then I suggest you go find someone stronger to snipe at!' She caught his look of stunned surprise and didn't care.

From what she already knew of him throwing his weight around was second nature. He had probably not been spoken to in such a way during the whole of his over-privileged life. In her opinion a reprimand was long overdue!

Filomena reached for her hand and gave it a warm squeeze and Cesare, on his dignity, announced, 'I apologise, Nonna. I have been anxious. Now I will go and arrange round the clock nursing care.'

He turned, his shoulders rigid, but was held back by his grandmother saying, 'I forbid it. I will not have strangers fussing around me and doing objectionable things to me! I am not ill. I simply need to rest until I am mended. Jilly and Rosa will tend me between them.'

He turned back then. Slowly. His dark eyes sought Milly's. 'You are capable?'

Her chin came up. She returned the pressure of the old lady's fingers. 'Perfectly.' Her dark green gaze steady, she held her breath. Would he back down or would he, after her insubordination, insist on hiring nursing staff?

They weren't to know it but the real Jilly would run a mile rather than put a foot one inch inside a sickroom. She had no patience with what she perceived as weakness in anyone.

He was watching her through hooded eyes, as if doubting her capability, and was about to offer up some argument that would allow him to get his own way. It was time for her to put her foot down again.

'Please ask Rosa to fix a lunch tray for your grandmother. Something light.' She turned to the old lady. 'A little soup, perhaps?' She received her amused nod and added firmly, 'And then she must rest.'

Did his savagely handsome mouth quirk? Milly wasn't sure and was not about to let herself think about it, not while she was desperate to stop herself from having any thoughts about him at all, especially after what he had made her feel this morning. How he had made her behave!

'You handle him well,' Filomena remarked as soon as the door had closed behind him. 'He has the habit of authority. Though well deserved, I am the first to admit. He is always right.'

She sounded tired and Milly wondered if she was brooding over his comment that she was not to be trusted to look where she was going. In her weakened state his snapped comment would have been upsetting.

'He adores you,' Milly was quick to console. 'He was only grumpy with you because you'd given him such a fright. It's a natural reaction.'

Had that first hot, savage kiss been born out of anger at the danger she'd unknowingly put herself in? Had it been a question of kiss her or shake her until her teeth fell out? Probably. And, as for what had happened next, well, he believed she was her sister, his ex-lover, and the progression had also been completely natural, that first punishing kiss rekindling old flames.

Nothing to do with her, Milly. Nothing personal.

Thankfully, Rosa appeared with a tray, taking her mind off such dejecting, demoralising thoughts. Settling it on the old lady's knees, murmuring in her own language, the housekeeper finally addressed Milly. 'Would you also like tray? Keep the *Signora* company?'

Breaking the soft bread roll that accompanied the broth and, buttering it, earning herself a smile of gratitude from her charge, Milly seized the offer. 'Thank you, Rosa. I think I'll take all my meals with the *Signora,* if it's no trouble.' That way she could avoid eating with Cesare. The less she could manage to see of him the better.

'*Di niente!*' The housekeeper beamed. 'Much good plan!'

In the event Milly saw hardly anything of Cesare except when he visited his grandmother at around ten each morning and again at ten in the evenings, or whenever the doctor appeared to check up on his patient. And on every occasion Milly made her excuses and left the room, only returning when she was sure the coast was clear. For the rest of the time Cesare was closeted in his first floor office, commanding his empire or occasionally visiting headquarters in Florence.

She wasn't being cowardly in avoiding him as much as possible, she assured herself. Just being sensible. She was in grave danger of believing herself in love with him. It was bad enough having him haunt her dreams at night—dreams so erotic she woke with a feeling of deep shame—without having to be in his company during waking hours.

It had been four weeks since Filomena's accident and the old lady was making great strides and Cesare had been away on business—Hong Kong and somewhere in the Far East, according to the patient—for the past ten days, apparently comfortable about leaving her in charge which, she supposed, was progress!

On the whole Milly was much easier than she'd been when she'd first arrived. Her duties were satisfying. She and Filomena were growing fonder of each other as each day passed and life here at the villa had settled into a pleasant routine.

But.

Her deception was really bugging her now. Deceiving a kind, trusting old lady was despicable—there was no other word for it and she was no nearer tracing her sister than she had been back in Ashton Lacey. And deceiving Cesare was every bit as distasteful.

She was going to have to come clean and take the flak, she decided with a sickening lurch of her stomach. Let Cesare with his wealth and clout find her sister and then they could finally get the misunderstanding cleared up and she could go home—providing Cesare didn't decide to prosecute her as well which, she decided miserably, was a high probability!

And, not nearly as important but still troublesome, she was heartily sick of having to wear Jilly's cast-offs. Everything was either too tight-fitting, too short, too low cut, too brashly in-your-face, or a mixture of all four! Whatever she wore she felt uncomfortable.

Putting her sour mood down to the cream leather miniskirt and matching sleeveless top—surely one of Jilly's impulse buys because it didn't seem to have been worn before—she collected secateurs from the garden room and headed across the cobbled courtyard on the spindly heels that were *de rigueur* as far as Jilly was concerned, apart from the weird sandals that had finally fallen to pieces during that last hurried scramble over the island to the helicopter.

Rosa was sitting with her mistress for a couple of hours, as she did each afternoon, and Milly would cut fresh roses for Filomena's room. She knew how much she enjoyed them, especially as she couldn't get out in the garden herself yet.

Soothed by the prospect of an hour in the beautiful gardens, she made her way through the formal box parterre, theatrical with its stone urns and magnifient central carved fountain, through the perfumed lemon grove and on to the path that led to what Filomena called her English garden, a yew enclosed area that was filled with her precious roses in generous beds edged with aromatic lavender.

After looking in on Nonna briefly and, having a word with Rosa to make sure his grandmother's steady progress was continuing, Cesare headed for his office and dumped his bulging briefcase. Loosening his tie, he allowed that he was more than glad to be home.

For the past few months he'd worked from home, or when necessary from the Florence office, feeling trapped, missing the dynamism of covering all the corners of his business empire in his private jet, the hands-on troubleshooting he thrived on.

It had been necessary, initially because of what he had seen as Nonna's worrying lack of interest in staying alive, and then because, although the young companion he'd hired had kept her amused, seemingly giving her a new lease of life, something had told him Jilly Lee couldn't be trusted.

And so he'd stayed home, his decision validated when he'd been left to pick up the pieces after the thieving little tramp had disappeared.

A problem to be solved at the Far East refinery followed by his unavoidable presence at the opening of the opulent retail outlet for the breathtakingly expensive Saracino gems had necessitated a stop-over in Hong Kong. Once a regular part of his focused—some said driven—working life, jetting between the various arms of his empire, making sure everything was working smoothly.

But instead of feeling free, enjoying doing what he did best, he had been itching to get back home.

Facing facts as he prided himself on doing, he wandered to the tall window that overlooked the courtyard, shedding his suit jacket on the way, ignoring the clatter of the fax machine.

Concern for his grandmother wasn't the reason—daily reports from Rosa had assured him that she was doing splendidly, that the companion, Signorina Jilly, was amazing all the staff by showing her gentler side, so much good humour and patience.

So even his staff had noted the startling change in character!

Put simply, he hadn't been able to get the bewitching little imposter out of his head. Remembering how her practically naked, perfectly lovely body had felt in his arms, her passionate, generous response, had been responsible for more sleepless nights than he wanted to think about.

And the way she had avoided him since they'd returned to the villa had had him wanting to punch holes in walls. He had to discover why she was pretending to be her much harder twin sister. Every time he'd decided to make her come clean something had happened to stop him. It was as if fate was conspiring against him. And the need to know was assuming monumental proportions.

Thrusting his hands into the side pockets of his narrow fitting suit trousers, he rocked back on his heels and told himself that her deliberate avoidance had forced a necessary and sensible patience on his behalf.

Have the whole thing out with her he would, but not until Nonna was fit again and back on her feet. There was always the danger that, when confronted with what he knew, had known for weeks, the imposter would run.

Short of locking her in her room and chaining her to the bedpost, there was little he could do to ensure that she didn't simply disappear. And he was honest enough to acknowledge that he had more reasons than one for not wanting that to happen.

He froze, the breath locking in his lungs as a savage stab of lustful sensation arrowed through him. The object of his serial thoughts had just entered the courtyard, heading for the garden room, judging by the flowers that were cradled in the crook of one arm.

She looked hot, uncomfortable. Pausing, she thrust out her lush lower lip and puffed out a breath to shift the now overlong silvery blonde fringe out of her eyes, then plucked crossly at the unsuitable tacky leather mini-skirt that showed far too much of her delec-table legs than was wise in company.

Just the sort of tasteless garment her twin would choose, he decided as she walked on, tottering on ridiculously high heels over the cobbles.

Cesare expelled a harsh breath and, lust ignored for the moment, decided on a pang of soft sympathy to do something for her. Re-trieving his mobile from his jacket pocket, he flipped it open and began to dial.

'They are beautiful, my dear,' Filomena enthused as Milly fed the last rose into place in the crystal bowl. 'How I miss my garden! It is so thoughtful of you to bring it to me.'

'It won't be long now,' Milly promised with a warm smile. Next week Filomena was due to have another X-ray and if the collar bone was healed she could be rid of the sling and could venture out of doors. Already she was able to walk around her room without discomfort, which showed her ribs were healing well, and she sat for several hours in the armchair by one of the tall windows. 'Now, would you like me to read to you?'

There was a shelf full of new books which, she learned, Jilly and Filomena had chosen in Florence—thankfully all English language editions because of the old lady's wish to thoroughly familiarise herself with the tongue she had learned as a young woman. They were currently halfway through Dickens's *A Christmas Carol,* Milly's choice because she'd been given a copy on her tenth birthday and had read it annually ever since, gradually acquiring all the great author's works.

'Later.' Dark eyes twinkled. 'We will talk now and you will tell me more about yourself. Especially about young men. I'm sure you must have someone special waiting for you back home.' She smiled with pure mischief. 'Most anxious to see you again—just as I'm sure your little sister must be!'

A bubble of hysteria burst in Milly's

stomach. So far nothing more had been said of the horrible suggestion that she invite her 'little sister' over for a holiday! What if her putative boyfriend were to be included in the invitation?'

Trying not to squawk in horror at the prospect, she tugged at the horrid leather top, which made her feel overheated and tacky, and denied, 'I don't have a boyfriend.' Which was the absolute truth.

The moment Cesare had left the premises for his headquarters in Florence a few days after they'd returned to the villa she'd phoned Bruce to stop him worrying about where she had got to and had received a far from interested or sympathetic reaction to her news that she was working in Tuscany for the time being as paid companion to a lovely Italian lady.

Words like *Inconsiderate... Flighty behaviour... Mother and I always thought you were steady and sensible... Disappointed in you...*

In the end she had put the phone down on

him, thanking her lucky stars that she had never regarded him as anything more than a friend, only being thrown in a loop when his mother had talked about formalising their so-called relationship.

'Now why do I find that so hard to believe?' Filomena questioned with a mischievous smile and Milly shifted uneasily in the chair she'd chosen to use, hating the way the leather skirt stuck to her thighs and made a discomfiting sucking noise when she moved and wishing she could kick off her silly shoes because her feet were killing her and wondering how Jilly could actually choose to wear such stuff.

Thankfully, when Cesare entered the room, she was spared more personal delving. She hadn't known he was back and, to her horror, a hot spiralling ache invaded her pelvis as she stared at his broad and gorgeous back and narrowly clad long legs as he immediately strode over to where his grandmother sat and lifted her hands to his lips, sparing Milly not a single glance.

Gratefully seizing the opportunity to make herself scarce, she got to her feet and, as if Cesare had second sight, he drawled, 'Stay where you are. I need to talk to you both.'

Turning, he caught her in the act of sneaking out of the room. Her face flushed a furious scarlet then paled to ash grey beneath the light tan she'd picked up since arriving in Tuscany when he announced, his fantastically handsome face the picture of innocence, 'Nonna, if you can spare Jilly, I need to be in Florence. I'd like to take her with me—I'm sure there are things she needs to buy and I'd like to give her dinner afterwards.'

As a bombshell it couldn't have been more unwelcome. She had no idea what he was up to. In her role as Jilly she should jump at the opportunity to spend time with her one-time lover, hoping against hope he could be persuaded to change his mind about marriage.

But as she wasn't her twin, merely her pale shadow—a shadow who craved his company as well as seeing the personal danger in that weak self indulgence—she would have to get out of it somehow.

She sent an unconsciously pleading look in Filomena's direction, willing the old lady to voice an objection at being deprived of her companion, and felt sickeningly let down when all she got was a bright smile and, 'What a splendid idea! I spoiled the break she needed when I had that silly accident and she has worked tirelessly and so cheerfully. A daughter couldn't have shown more kindness—she deserves to be spoiled!'

Milly cringed at the fulsome praise, she didn't deserve it, not while her deceit was sticking like a hard rock behind her breastbone. And there was no way out as far as she could see, not unless she threw a sudden fainting fit. As she didn't trust her acting ability to accomplish that she mumbled through a mouth that felt too stiff to open, 'I'll get changed, then.'

'There's no need.' Cesare was at her side. A firm hand encircled her arm, just above her elbow. Her flesh burned and quivered at his touch. It was the first time he had touched her since that morning on the beach and it sensitised every cell in her body, made her so sexually aware of him she didn't know what to do with herself.

'You can change later,' he promised silkily. 'Right now, Stefano is waiting to drive us.'

CHAPTER NINE

STARING AT THE back of Stefano's neck and thankful for the sleek, top-of-the-range vehicle's effective air-conditioning that helped her feel marginally less sticky and uncomfortable, Milly vowed that the moment she and Cesare got some privacy she would come clean, tell him everything and take his understandable and flaying anger because she guessed she deserved it.

Gritting her teeth, she tried to ignore the bombardment of nerves that was turning her stomach upside down and inside out at the thought that after his initial rage would come his scornful hatred. She tried to concentrate on figuring out why Cesare, cool and brooding and speechless at her side, had insisted she go to Florence with him and what he had meant when he'd told her she could change later.

She would have asked him there and then but she positively knew she wouldn't get the whole truth, just something bland, fit for Stefano's ears.

When the car at last drew to a halt in front of the Saracino Palace she stared at the opulent Renaissance building with wide-eyed awe. During one of her long chatty conversations with Filomena the old lady had mentioned in passing that the hotel had been in their family for decades, as if it was no big deal!

Unable to imagine what it must be like to belong to a family that had old money coming out of its ears—not to mention the gigantic profits that came from a world-spanning business empire, Milly settled to wait as Cesare fired off instructions in Italian to Stefano and slid his long legs to the pavement, imagining that perhaps she was to be dropped somewhere else in the city and returned at an hour of Cesare's choosing.

But the door at her side swung open and she found herself staring into that darkly sexy face, her stomach flipping as he commanded with impatience at her glued to her seat stance, 'Come, we are blocking the traffic.'

'I'm sorry, I thought—'

'*Basta!* Just move it!'

Only now aware of the cacophony of car horns Milly slid out, appalled by the way her borrowed miniskirt skidded up to reveal her no-nonsense white panties, flushing to the roots of her pale blonde hair as someone vented a loud wolf-whistle. Her colour in no way subsided as Cesare clamped a lean bronzed hand on her elbow and hustled her on to the pavement as a uniformed doorman gave him a deferential greeting.

Respect and genuine warmth enveloped him on all sides, Milly noted as he strode with her over the cool marble paving of the immense reception area. She was horribly aware of the same eyes assessing her, though.

His staff probably thought she was some slapper he'd picked up off the street and, her slim shoulders slumping as she tried to make herself invisible, she muttered uncomfortably, 'I'm not dressed for this place and if you're thinking of eating here—' he had told Filomena he wanted to give her dinner '—I'd rather find a back street joint,' and found herself ushered into a private lift and whisked upwards.

Cesare, leaning back against the satin finished steel wall, studied her through veiled eyes. The blonde silk of her hair tumbled into her eyes and her lovely mouth was a mutinous pink pout and she winced whenever she took a step in the ridiculous heels she was wearing. His heart ached for her discomfort and he marvelled at the feeling of guilt that consumed him over what was to come.

Telling her he was fully aware that she was not who she was pretending to be would shame and embarrass her and he hated the thought of that, of doing or saying anything to hurt or discomfit her, and tried to make sense of the immense protective feelings she aroused in him. Shifting his position uneasily he hoped he wasn't turning soft, losing his edge!

But it had to be done, he reminded himself with cool determination as the doors whispered open directly on to the sitting room of the elegant suite kept exclusively for his use.

Milly's spiky heels sank into the depth of the soft jade-green carpet that covered a vast room in which a group of pale lemon silk-covered upholstered armchairs surrounded a long low marble-topped table, the rest of the furniture being ornate antiques, the Tuscan landscapes on the silk-covered walls framed with gilded opulence.

'This suite is kept for my use,' he imparted coolly, slapping down his libido and ignoring the growing need to kiss her again, to discover if she would respond as beautifully as she had on that never to be forgotten occasion. 'And for the use of important clients or occasional business colleagues.'

Had he brought Jilly here? Had he insisted on conducting their affair away from the prying eyes of his grandmother and his staff at the villa? A shiver coursed through her and only stopped when she got her brain into gear and remembered that he thought she was Jilly and if he'd brought her here before he wouldn't be making those explanations.

This ridiculous and utterly hateful situation had to end! Gathering all her courage, her confession on the tip of her tongue, her eyes shot to his as he forestalled her. 'I have something for you.'

His eyes were warm—she would have said tender had she been in the habit of giving way to wild imaginings. And his smile made her forget what she'd been going to say as he led her through to a sumptuous bedroom where half a dozen classy boxes were laid out on the satin coverlet of the enormous half tester bed.

'I had these delivered. Replacements for the

clothes you left behind on the island in your desire to waste not one moment because you understood my haste to fly to Nonna's side. I hope you approve, I explained your size and your characteristics in detail.'

He sounded like a sultan bestowing favours on the newest member of his harem, she thought wildly, and just knew the boxes would contain thongs, miniskirts and see-through tops, the sort of overtly sexy stuff Jilly went for—all singing, all dancing, look-at-me stuff!

A hand in the small of her back he edged her forwards, towards the bed, but she dug her heels in and said, 'I can't take them!' And then, because that sounded really ungrateful because he obviously believed he'd been doing her—Jilly—a favour and no one liked having their generosity and good intentions shoved back at them, she amended, 'It was a nice thought but I can't take them.' She dragged in a huge breath and got out in a rush, 'I'm not Jilly. I'm her twin sister. I'm sorry to have deceived you, but I did have my reasons.'

For a long moment Cesare found it impossible to articulate a single word for the flood of relief that took his breath away. Many signs had told him that she was deeply uncomfortable with the situation she had put herself in—or her twin had forced her into—but finally she had found the courage to tell him the truth and saved him from having to accuse her. He admired her for that. More than admired her? He shelved that question and studied her instead.

Her long lashes veiled the brilliance of her eyes as she stared at the floor and her face was pale, her shoulders tense as if she were expecting a blow. Or his anger.

Quick to disabuse her of that expectation, he put a gentle forefinger beneath her chin and lifted her face to his.

Her colour returned in a flood. Milly felt it in the hot burn of her skin as she met the steady intensity of those dark-as-night eyes and dizziness almost overwhelmed her as he announced softly, 'I know, Milly. I began to have suspicions almost as soon as we reached the villa from England. They were confirmed by telephone on the following morning just before we set out for the island. Jilly Lee had an identical twin, Milly.'

'Oh!' Her heart began to pound and her knees turned to unset jelly. 'Why? Why didn't you—?'

'Say something?' he supplied and, placing a steadying arm around her waist, he led her to a white velvet upholstered chaise and watched while she sank on to it with every appearance of wishing the floor would open up and swallow her. 'I made a mental date on several occasions to hit you with what I knew but something always happened to make me hold back.' He folded his lean powerful length on to the seat beside her and a smile warmed his voice to smooth honey. 'And in retrospect I'm glad. My first intention was to let you stew during that first day on the island

and then come down on you like several tons of bricks. Had I done so I would not have discovered how unlike your twin you really are.'

'I don't understand,' Milly said strickenly, her breath catching in her throat. He was so close that the spicy, faintly lemony, husky male scent of him was in her nostrils; it made every nerve-ending in her body quiver. She felt punch drunk by his proximity and knew she shouldn't.

A tiny whimper of distress escaped her and Cesare sprang to his feet and strode out of the room, so lithe and graceful he made her heart ache, and she didn't know whether to be grateful because the raging anger she'd braced herself to meet hadn't materialised or whether to curl up with smothering humiliation because all the time he'd known she wasn't Jilly and must have been laughing his silk socks off at her useless attempts to pretend she was.

Returning moments later, Cesare put a glass into her hands, closing her fingers around the cut crystal bowl. 'A little brandy. You are in shock, I think.'

He sounded so damned complacent! Milly tossed the fiery liquid back and a rare upsurge of rage had her blurting, 'So all the time you were laughing at me! Watching me make a fool of myself! I hate you!'

'No, you don't,' Cesare stated with infuriating calm and prised the empty glass from her tense fingers. 'Whatever emotions you have inspired in me, mirth wasn't one of them. I admit to being as furious as an angry bull when I first had my suspicions confirmed. That changed to interest. Why had you stepped into your twin's shoes—quite literally—when you are so unlike each other?'

'Not so!' Milly contradicted, the effect of the alcohol in her bloodstream making her reckless. 'We wear our hair differently, that's all. Jilly would never wear hers short, but you weren't to know that.'

'Superficially you look alike, providing one scrapes away the layers of make-up your sister uses. But deep down, where it matters, you are astonishingly different.' On that assurance, he cupped her flushed face with both hands. 'Jilly is hard, self centred. Manipulative. Charming when it serves her purpose but insincere. She flaunts her sex to get what she wants. That makes her ugly.'

The balls of his thumbs stroked her delicate cheekbones and Milly's heart missed a beat then turned over, making her forget what she'd been about to say in her sister's defence as he continued. 'You are beautiful. You are warm and gentle, caring. Yet unafraid to speak your mind if you think someone else has suffered an injustice—as you rebuked me, quite rightly, when my recent anxiety made me speak sharply to my grandmother. I admire that. That is the difference that sticks out a thousand miles.'

Glorying in the touch of his hands, heat curling deep in her pelvis, her nipples shamingly prominent, it was all Milly could do to stop herself from hurling herself at him, hold him close, beg him to kiss her.

She had to remind herself very vigorously that he was merely being kind to someone who'd just been shocked to learn she'd been the biggest fool in Christendom. Showing him that she wanted him quite desperately would only make her look an even bigger fool in his eyes than she already did!

'Now—' his hands left her face as he unfurled his impressive length and rose to his feet '—all this must have been difficult for you. Come—' he took her hand and urged her to her feet '—you will shower and change into something more suited to you and then we will eat and you will explain why you felt it necessary to impersonate your sister.'

Loving the feel of his strong fingers as they curled around her own, and despising herself for that weakness, Milly allowed herself to be escorted to the bed. 'Choose what you would like to change into,' he suggested, hitting the nail on the head with the shrewdness she was beginning to expect from him when he added,

'You clearly are not comfortable in your sister's choice of clothing.'

That comment needed no reply but Milly's hands were unsteady as, at his prompting, she opened the nearest box and gasped as Cesare plucked a dream of a dress from the tissue layers. Delicate voile in subtle soft stripes of oyster and pale pink, it had a discreet V neckline, a slightly bloused bodice and a soft flowing skirt below the neat waistline. It was just the sort of dress she would have bought herself had she ever been remotely able to afford to do so.

Quelling her excitement as further goodies were revealed—tailored linen trousers, cream-coloured and light charcoal, elegant shirts, cool filmy skirts and tops, shoes with neat kitten heels, delicate fine cotton underwear hand-embroidered with pretty sprays of forget-me-nots—Milly felt deeply regretful as she stressed, 'I can't possibly accept all this.'

'But of course you can.' Cesare swept her

objection aside with a downward slash of one long-fingered hand. 'Look on these things as payment in lieu of wages.'

'You said I had to work for nothing,' she reminded him sternly because so far he had held the moral high ground and she was determined to snatch some of it for herself. Gentle and caring in his eyes—although she had never looked at herself in that light—but a doormat she most certainly wasn't!

But as usual he had an unassailable comeback. 'I made that stipulation when I believed I had cornered your sister. You are not your sister. You have put in the hours caring for my grandmother. Reading to her, chatting, bringing her flowers, taking her mind away from her injuries. I wouldn't expect anyone to work for my family for nothing. I suggest you take that shower and get out of that thing you are wearing.'

Cesare turned away. The temptation to take that tacky apology for a skirt off her, strip the tight-fitting matching leather top from her lovely body and join her in the shower was overwhelming. An over-active libido? Or something else?

Milly had given up trying to figure him out. Basically he was a good man. He cared for his staff, was always polite and considerate in his dealings with them and he adored the grandmother who'd brought him up after he'd been orphaned. So, knowing she wasn't the twin who stood accused of theft in his eyes, he had been kind to her, mostly, especially after he'd decided not to come down on her like several tons of bricks.

It really puzzled her. And it was pointless trying to figure it out and tying her brain in knots, she decided as she stepped out of the most welcome shower she'd ever taken in her life.

Wrapping herself in one of the huge fluffy bath sheets, a different thought struck her like a bolt of lightning and robbed her of the ability to breathe, to move.

When he'd started to make love to her it hadn't been because he believed she was his ex-lover as she'd thought. He'd known she wasn't!

It was she, Milly, who'd turned him on!

Her gaze met her reflection in one of the floor to ceiling mirrors and her heart jumped. Her eyes looked huge, sparkling and her mouth looked swollen, soft, as if she'd just been kissed to within an inch of her life.

Smothering an internal groan she turned away and began to towel dry her hair with startling vigour. She wasn't going to go there! It was a non-starter of a track, ending nowhere!

She would just enjoy feeling fresh and clean, her skin perfumed with the fragrant body lotion she had found and was using lavishly. She slipped on the pretty undies and the dream of a dress, which fitted her to per-fection and made her look cool, classy and strangely elegant—a far cry from the way she'd presented herself in Jilly's cast-offs.

Locating a comb on the dressing table, she

ran it through her silky hair and was ready. Taking a deep breath, she stepped into the pair of oyster-coloured butter-soft leather kitten heels she'd selected and walked to the *en suite* bathroom door, ready now to do her utmost to convince Cesare that Jilly wasn't a thief, that there must have been some terrible mistake. To beg him to try to trace her whereabouts because she was growing increasingly anxious for her vanished twin's well-being.

As she entered the bedroom Cesare appeared in the doorway that led to the sitting room.

He had shed his suit jacket and his silk tie and there was a tension about the broad shoulders beneath the fine white cotton of his shirt. After a timeless head to toe scrutiny his eyes held hers for what seemed to Milly like long breathless moments, as if he could reach into her soul and read it.

And then he smiled. Slow and devastating. And commanded, his voice thick, 'Come here.'

CHAPTER TEN

MILLY WENT LIKE a sleepwalker, something in the depths of those fathomless dark eyes, something slow, burning and impossible to resist, was drawing her to him.

Her whole body unbearably sensitized, she stood before him, felt the heat of him, the firm caress of his hands as they settled on either side of her tiny waist.

Lush ebony lashes veiled the gleam in his eyes and his voice was a purr of masculine appreciation as he murmured, *'Bella, bella! La direttrice* understood my directions perfectly.' Then, the line of his gorgeous mouth wry with a hint of amusement, 'Forgive me. Not one word of my native language must be spoken because you do not understand it! It was the first test I ran, weeks ago, and it heightened the suspicions I was already having.'

Cesare's thumbs were rotating seductively against her ribcage, the wicked sensation making her breath tremble in her lungs, her breasts surge in urgent invitation for his touch against the confines of her pretty flower-sprigged bra. Her rosy flush had nothing to do with the humiliation of knowing that she hadn't fooled him for more than a handful of hours and everything to do with her fierce hunger for him.

His hands had worked their way upwards and tension held her very still. Burningly expectant. Another fraction of an inch and his seductive hands would be touching the under-swell of her breasts.

Barely containable excitement rippled down the length of her narrow spine and heat pooled wildly between her thighs as she willed with everything she had for his hands to move that fraction higher. Then, his voice oddly hoarse, he promised, 'I will teach you my language. It will be a pleasure for both of us.'

At mind-blowing speed Milly came crashing to her senses, straight back down to earth.

What was he talking about? And what on earth did she think she was doing? Teach her his language? When? Did he expect her to stay on? As Filomena's companion, even though that dear old lady would surely despise her for her deceit? Or because he fancied her, as he had briefly fancied Jilly, so she would be handy whenever he got the impulse to invite her to share his bed?

Pushing small hands against the hard breadth of his chest she swung away. Wrapping her arms around her midriff to stop herself from trembling, she clenched her teeth and gritted, 'We need to talk about my sister, remember?'

'We do?' He sounded lightly amused as he positioned himself to stand behind her, his hands on her shoulders, fingers touching the bare flesh of her upper arms.

He touched his long sensual mouth to the pale hollow where her neck met her shoulder and she shuddered with forbidden delight and made herself resist the febrile temptation to turn, wrap her arms around his neck and beg for his kiss.

'You hurt her badly,' she pronounced baldly. She paced a step away from him, away from the danger of him. 'That's my educated guess.'

'Tell me about it.' He sounded genuinely perplexed. He was one class act, Milly reminded herself, he was a twenty-four carat womaniser. If she'd been weak enough to join in his no doubt standard seduction routine, then by now he would have been undressing her, and she would have been helping him, destination that handy big bed with no thought of future heartbreak, no thought except her consuming need for him.

Would it have given him a kick to notch up both twins?

Would she have welcomed his love-making because she loved him?

The thought appalled her, made her speech-less so that Cesare had to prompt, 'So tell me about your educated guess.'

The arrival of room service gave her breathing space, allowing her to piece together her fragmented wits while the slim young waiter whisked the trolley through tall windows that led out to a balcony.

'We can talk while we eat.' A hand in the small of her back propelled her over the sea of jade green and out on to the balcony that overlooked secluded gardens that gave up the heady perfume of jasmine into the dusky air.

Holding out a chair for her at the small round table he promised huskily, 'And after talking, who knows?'

Milly closed her ears to that! And shivered slightly despite the warmth of the evening air. At his invitation, she helped herself to a little of this, a little of that, of what exactly she couldn't have said because she was far too wound up to even think of eating.

A healthy gulp of the crisp, sparkling and

delicious champagne gave her the impetus to state, 'Jilly isn't a thief. My guess is she only disappeared because you'd hurt her so badly. The last time we heard from her was when she wrote and told us she was leaving her job as a receptionist—at least I think it was a receptionist, I don't remember exactly—at a high class nightclub here in Florence. She didn't say where she was going or what she'd be doing, only that she would soon be able to pay back every penny she owed our mother.'

She levelled an accusing glance at him and stabbed a prawn as if she were wishing she could stab the fork into him. 'She obviously believed everything was coming good. We had no idea she'd moved in with you, acting as your grandmother's companion. She must have met you before, here in Florence, I would imagine. You were lovers and I guess she believed you and she would be married.'

Another throat cooling draught of champagne, then, 'When she realised that wasn't going to happen she left, broken-hearted.' She shot him a darkly glittering look. 'I know she'd never been in love before. She'd had loads of boyfriends. They didn't seem able to resist her, from what she told us. But never anyone serious for her. Except you, apparently. And you only wanted one thing. And that was sex,' she spelled out with brutal frankness.

She set the glass down with a mini crash. 'There has to be some misunderstanding about the theft. And I want you to undo some of the damage and help me find her.' Her mouth wobbled. 'I'm getting really worried about her. And she doesn't even know—' the wobble got serious '—that Ma died.'

'*Cara.*' Cesare leaned across the table, his eyes intent on her troubled features. 'I hate to see you upset. We will find her, I promise you. Already the search is well in hand.'

'It is?' A slight frown appeared between her eyes.

'But of course.' He leaned back again, relaxed, exuding male confidence.

'But of course,' she parroted as the penny

dropped with a decided clang, an edge of bitterness in her tone. 'Oh, silly me! You know, I only decided to step into Jilly's shoes to stop you hounding her, to give her time to get over the way you must have treated her, let her get her act together so she'd be fit to speak in her own defence. But the moment you knew I wasn't who I was pretending to be the search was back on.'

Across the table the slight elevation of one ebony brow infuriated her. She shot to her feet. 'Take me back to the villa. It's getting late.' Her chin came up, her deep green eyes glinting with intent. 'I'll stay with Filomena until she's back to normal—provided she wants me to when she learns who I really am—and then I'm off and you can hire another companion.' It was the only way. She was really stupid and in grave danger of falling for a serial womaniser. Stay around him and she'd end up as broken-hearted as her twin.

'Nonna doesn't expect us to return tonight.' The bald statement stopped her in her tracks. Oh, the rat! He had brought her here, had supplied her with a whole wardrobe of lovely new clothes, a fancy meal which she'd hardly touched, plied her with champagne, all with the intention of seducing her! Her face burned, hot as a furnace.

He had stationed himself in the doorway to the interior of the suite, blocking her way. She faced him. 'Is this your normal routine? Shower your prey with pretty gifts, promise marriage and access to untold wealth, then walk away when you get bored!' She took a deep breath, her tone as icy as she could make it. 'Let me pass.'

Dusk was deepening to night but she could see the slight flare of his nostrils, denoting anger. Well, tough. No man—especially a man as all-fired self confident and proud as Cesare Saracino—liked to have his faults rammed down his throat.

'I don't need a routine and I don't recall asking you to marry me,' he sliced back at her. His hands shot out to fasten on her forearms.

'And there are a few things we ought to straighten out as it seems I'm to be cast as the bad guy,' he announced grimly. 'First and foremost, since it seems to be your priority, your twin was traced to a nightclub in this city. Where she worked as a so-called hostess, not a receptionist—no mention of that dubious occupation was made in her CV. No one had heard from her since she left, and the consensus was that no one cared. She was not well liked. Enquiries were made at the London store—supposedly the last full time job she held before she came to Italy—and again blanks were drawn. Her former colleagues hadn't cared enough about her to want to keep in touch. Since then the investigation has returned to Italy. I'm sorry,' he added more temperately as he felt the fight drain out of her. 'Jilly may attract a certain type of man, but among women she is far from popular.'

Trying to get her head round what he was telling her, that her dazzling, outgoing sister

was actively disliked by her female colleagues, she failed to resist when Cesare
slipped an arm around her waist and walked
her back into the living room.

Settling her into one of the armchairs, he sat
on the arm of the adjacent one, the light from
the overhead chandelier burnishing his raven-
dark hair, throwing the sculpted bones of his
spectacularly handsome face into hard masculine relief.

Milly averted her eyes. He was so beautiful,
so tempting. She hated what he was implying
about her twin and yet she still wanted him
and she had to find some way of defending
Jilly, but—

'There can be no doubt about the signatures
on the cheques she cashed,' Cesare said flatly.
'A handwriting expert confirmed what I
believed. They were forgeries.' Forcing
himself to ignore the way her delicate skin
lost all colour, he stated, 'And, just for the
record, I was never her lover.'

At that Milly straightened her spine. 'You

as good as admitted it,' she reminded him thickly. 'Once, early on, I addressed you as Signor Saracino and you made some snide comment about my not being so formal when I came to your bed!' Her eyes defied him but she felt sick inside. If he'd lied about that he could have been lying about everything else.

'True.' A strong hand cupped her chin, forcing her to keep looking at him, and his voice softened. 'I will not repeat the crude words she used when she appeared uninvited and unclad in my bedroom. That is what I was referring to when I still believed you were your twin. But I will tell you that I told her to get out of my sight in double quick time or she was out of a job—regardless of how Nonna had come to rely on her company. I was heartily sick of her coming on to me. I was not, and never could be, interested. Soon after that, no doubt realising she was on a loser, she disappeared. And a few days later, while doing Nonna's accounts I noticed a couple of large withdrawals to cash. The rest you know.'

Milly closed her eyes to hide the sudden sting of tears. Her emotions were all over the place. She had been fighting it but now she knew she had to believe him. He had no need to lie.

But Jilly—it hurt her immeasurably, but she had the horrible feeling that everything he'd said to her twin's detriment was no less than the truth.

Seeing her sister through unblinkered eyes, she had no option but to acknowledge that Jilly had taken their mother's nest-egg, her only safety net, and had lost every penny and much more. Then those careless, airy promises to pay it back, something that had never even begun to materialise, her thoughtlessness in rarely contacting them, as if they didn't matter, as if their having to live in a mean rented flat in severely reduced circumstances because they'd had to pay off the huge debts she'd incurred was nothing to do with her.

How she had always boasted that she could get any man she wanted. No problem.

But not this man!

The words echoed through her mind like an anthem of thanksgiving. And this man was stroking away an escaping tear with the ball of his thumb and she was choking with emotions she couldn't put a name to, but they were real and shatteringly strong.

'I'm sorry to have upset you, *cara*. But for my own sake it had to be said.'

For his sake? Too fraught to resist or even think about doing so, Milly found him standing over her, drawing her to her feet, into his gently enfolding arms.

She could have moved away if she'd wanted to. But she didn't. She felt safe.

'You've always hero-worshipped your sister,' Cesare guessed astutely, marvelling at his self-restraint in the way he was holding her when he ached to kiss every wonderful inch of her. But for her sake he knew he had to wait until she came to terms with her relationship problems with her sister.

'Yes, I suppose I have.' She held her bright head back to meet the warm concern in his eyes, her own cloudy, he noted on a tide of protective warmth. 'She was always the stronger character.'

Bossy, he mentally translated.

'She looked out for me when we were growing up and told me to always go to her if there were problems with other kids—like bullying—and she'd sort it.'

Thereby ensuring she was the dominant one, making sure she stayed that way, he assessed, pretty sure that the selfish Jilly wouldn't do anything without an ulterior motive, his hands taking on a will of their own and softly caressing her slim back.

'She could stand up to Dad,' Milly remembered quietly. 'He was a bit of a control freak and she couldn't always get her own way with him. But she could with Ma—she could twist her round her little finger.' Much to their mother's financial impoverishment, she thought with a stab of anger as she remembered the way they'd had to scratch and scrape to pay the rent and buy food.

Then, as if to make up for the ferocity of that thought, she confided shakily, 'When you appeared threatening prosecution I had to go ahead with—' her voice faltered, then gathered strength '—I had to do what I could to help her. We are twins and, believe me, whatever her faults there's a very strong bond.'

A bond that went one way only, Cesare amended savagely, but held his tongue, promising instead, 'When she's found, and she will be, I won't drag her through the courts, if it will please you. But I'll give her such a fright that never again will she be tempted to develop sticky fingers.'

Milly closed her eyes on a rush of relief. She trusted him to keep his word. Jilly might be careless with other people's money, careless when it came to keeping in touch with her family, dishonest—but maybe she'd been really desperate. It didn't excuse what she'd done—but she was her sister and she still couldn't bear to think of her having to face a prison sentence.

'Just one other thing—' She felt the warm

brush of his lips on first one eyelid and then the other and she whimpered low in her throat in weakening response and dragged in a jerk of breath as he told her, 'I had those clothes delivered because I knew you weren't comfortable in the sort of gear your sister wore. And I didn't bring you here to seduce you, though I do admit to being very tempted.'

Her eyes flew open at that admission and locked on to the undisguised hot desire in his. She was shaken to the core as she realised that only this man had ever, could ever, awaken such a hunger in her that she would be trembling on the brink of taking everything he could offer, giving back everything she was, and to hell with the consequences.

'And you, too, are tempted.' His seductive hands caressed her swollen breasts with breathtaking tenderness and her breath fluttered in her throat as she fought to control her desperate craving for him, snatching at a fast receding memory of the way she used to be— the glamorous Jilly's out-of-focus, boringly sensible shadow—just to get her feet back down to earth again.

'I think this shouldn't be happening,' she managed, almost disintegrating as fire burned low in her pelvis, mortified by her almost manic need to drag his clothes off. Her face glowed scarlet at the novel wanton thought. He touched his mouth to hers, his lips brushing hers lightly as he murmured, 'Feel with your heart; don't think with your head.'

Exactly where the danger lay! She felt light-headed, her entire body aching with powerful sexual awareness, and she had to scratch around for something to bring her back to her senses and finally managed unevenly, her breath melding with his as his mouth continued to tease and torment her, 'You forget, I am not my sister.'

His head came up, his stunning eyes holding hers as he denied, 'I forget nothing, *cara mia*. If you were your sister I would not be here. I would not be wanting you as I have never wanted any woman.'

His hands slid down to her narrow waist as he eased her closer to make her discover for herself exactly how much he wanted her and, ignoring her gasp, he elaborated, his voice thickening, 'Stop comparing yourself unfavourably to her. 'You are beautiful in a way she could never be. It comes from within you. She is base metal, you are pure gold. Remember that.'

His words filled her head until she felt dizzy. All of her life people had rated Jilly above her. She didn't think anyone had meant to, but when her sister walked into a room, a flash of bright colour, a stream of animated chatter, she dominated the space, all attention fixed on her.

Without a jealous bone in her body, Milly had always accepted her subordinate position as a fact of life that had no hope of changing. But now—now this fantastically charismatic, sexy man actually put her first!

Something twisted tightly inside her. She trembled violently and coiled her arms around his neck, knowing she had fallen in love with him and not afraid, now, to recognise that fact. It was a glorious, heady feeling and she would never regret it, even though she knew he would never feel the same way.

Both his hands snaked up to the back of her head, his fingers deep in the soft brightness of her silken hair as he bent his mouth to hers, lightly at first, a mere brush of butterfly wings against her quivering lips, and then as those lips parted the pressure increased and his tongue sought and found hers. He felt her body go up in flames as she kissed him back with all the fervour of an addict and he was lost, he who never lost himself, was drowning in this perfect woman.

He drew back, closing his eyes as her body squirmed with wanton eagerness against his, and said thickly, 'I burn for you.'

Her response was a mew of pleasure, the exploration of her small hands beneath the shirt that had somehow become unbuttoned. A shudder of driven need raked through him as he lifted her in his arms and strode with her to the bedroom beyond.

CHAPTER ELEVEN

THE ARRIVAL OF Room Service woke Milly from the scant two hours of slumber she'd managed; she had fallen asleep with the dawn in Cesare's strong arms.

She knew instantly that she was alone in the wildly rumpled bed and she could see morning sunlight behind her closed eyelids but was reluctant to acknowledge the waiter, to face the day that would surely have Cesare making arrangements for her return to England because, without doubt, Filomena would not waste time in seeing the back of her.

And much as he might have preferred her to stay on at the villa, available until he decided he wanted to hunt in pastures new, he would always bow to his beloved grandmother's wishes. Much as that reminder turned her sick inside, she knew a swift departure, a clean break and no regrets on her part would be for the best. The thought of leaving him now was pretty near unendurable. How much worse would it be if she stayed on as his lover for weeks, maybe even months?

So she would remain in her drowsy state for just a little while longer and blissfully relive every ecstatic moment of the most wonderful night of her life with Cesare, the man who had lodged himself firmly in her heart for all time.

She would never regret a single precious moment of their closeness, she vowed as she turned over and buried her face in the pillow and she would never forget him, what he meant to her.

She'd been an obvious novice to start with but Cesare had been so patient, his tenderness bringing tears to her eyes and making her love for him assume massive proportions. When he'd turned away to use protection it had given her pause as she'd wondered if he'd been that sure of making a conquest.

But that small doubt had vanished like morning mist, blown away by her sensible thought that he was simply being careful. He wouldn't want a pregnancy, though she wouldn't mind having his child. In truth she would welcome his child with all of her being. The difficulties of being a single parent would be as nothing beside the joy of having part of him with her for always.

Then even that thought had been blasted into orbit as he'd turned back to her, parting her thighs and trailing tiny kisses up the quivering length of them until her mind had been blown to pieces as he'd found the secret, damp heart of her femininity.

Her entire body glowed beneath the thin covering as she recalled how, after that first shatteringly magical time, she hadn't been able to get enough of him, all untutored eagerness that she recalled now with a secret cat-like smile, had seemed to drive him wild.

'*Cara.*' A kiss on her naked shoulder had her snaking round to feast her eyes on him, her sleep-flushed features wreathed with a smile of loving welcome.

His midnight hair was wet from the shower, his bronzed skin spangled with water droplets and his only covering was a towel hooked around his lean hips.

Her eyes limpid with adoration, Milly raised her arms to him, marvelling at the way daylight did nothing to dispel the intoxicating intimacy of the night hours as the sheet fell away to reveal breasts that were tight and swollen, aching for his touch.

Dark colour banded his sculpted cheek-bones as he sank down on the bed beside her, took her hands and muttered raggedly, 'You are an invitation that's hard to resist! However,' he released her hands and reached to the night table, handing her a bowl-like cup of coffee and announced prosaically, 'I need to head back to the villa, speak with my PA and call a meeting of all heads of department in New York for next week.'

Instead of offering her hot coffee he might just as well have doused her with icy water, Milly mourned, regretful that something that had been so wonderful for her was, for him, obviously an interlude that could be so easily blanked out, his world-spanning business empire uppermost in his mind, everything back to normal. The earth-shattering intimacies of the night were forgotten in the light of day with a single-minded masculine drive to get on with the important things of his life.

Was that what happened after a one night stand?

With her free hand she tugged the sheet up to conceal her nakedness. How was she to know? She had never played that game before and didn't know the rules. At least she had more pride than to whine and cling, and 'back to normal' raised a knotty problem.

Avoiding his stunning eyes because they always robbed her of her dwindling reserves of common sense, she asked, 'What do I tell Filomena? She'll be so upset to know she's been the victim of a con-trick. I don't want to go on deceiving her—I've felt truly bad about it.' Distress flooded her voice. 'But I will, just for a week or two, if you think we should keep the truth from her until she's properly well again.' She raised her eyes at last. 'What do you think?'

'I think…' he said slowly, lush ebony lashes not hiding the warm golden gleam in the eyes that could reduce her to a quivering state of absolute longing in the space of a single millisecond. A smile played now on his beautiful sensual mouth. 'I think that we should tell her that you are to be my wife.'

In a state of deep shock, her soft mouth fell open and her skin crawled with hot colour. 'Be serious,' she demanded unsteadily. As a joke it wasn't funny; it wasn't funny at all!'

In reply Cesare took the untouched coffee from her nerveless fingers, replaced it beside his on the night table, then took her hands in his. 'I have never been more serious in my entire life, *amore,*' he vowed softly, lifting her hands, his lips grazing her knuckles. 'I want you. Your exquisite body, your gentle heart. I want it all—the whole package. To be able to care for you, protect you, adore you, cherish you and spoil you. To be your husband, to give you my children.'

Her eyes widening, Milly shook her head slightly. Was she dreaming? How could the most wonderful man in the whole world want her to be his wife?

She put out an unsteady hand to touch his face, her fingers trailing over one high proud cheekbone, the hollow beneath, the corner of his so sexy mouth, trying to convince herself that this was real and not some fantasy born of her overwhelming love for him.

'Say yes!' His voice was demanding, his accent thickening, yet there was a trace of uncertainty there and it astonished her more than anything and sent her heart racing.

Then his mouth was on hers and his kiss

ravished her until she was incandescent with need and her, 'Yes, oh yes! Cesare, I love you—so much, so very much!' brought his head up, his chin at a proud angle. He promised, 'You will never regret this, *amore mia*.' His hands on her slim shoulders he held her away from him. 'And now, much as I regret it, we have to dress. Stefano will be here in thirty minutes to drive us back to the villa.'

Bestowing one swift slashing smile on her, he stood up, dropped the towel and strode in his glorious nakedness to a chest of drawers, pulling out garments at seeming random. His physique was so perfect it took her breath away and, unable to move a muscle, filled with such excitement that she thought she might explode from an overdose of happiness, she excused his ability to snap back in an instant to the business at hand.

Getting the job done was his modus operandi and she could live with that, she decided meltingly as he told her, 'On second thoughts, *cara mia*—and provided you agree—we will not tell Nonna of our marriage plans until she is perfectly well and strong again.' He pulled on a pair of light grey chinos and fastened the button at his lean waist, imparting, 'Knowing my stubborn grandmother and her joy to see me marrying at last, she will immediately start planning the service, the reception, the guest list, the flowers and your wardrobe. An earthquake wouldn't stop her. And in her present state of health it would prove to be too much. Do you understand what I mean?'

'Of course!' Milly's eyes sparkled with love at his consideration. And what did it matter if the wedding announcement was delayed for a couple of weeks?

'*Grazie*—thank you!' His smile dazzled her. He fastened the buttons of a black silk shirt. 'Besides, I will be overseas—a business trip that, alas, I cannot cancel—it will keep me away for several weeks. When I return we will share our news. And, as for Nonna and what she will think when you tell her who you are, do not trouble yourself, *mi amore*. She already knows.'

'She does!' At that shattering information Milly sat bolt upright, her eyes very wide.

'Indeed.' He was tying a silver-coloured silk tie. 'I told her before we came here and about your sister's theft. She was not surprised. In fact, when I explained that I was bringing you to the Saracino Palace to finally bring things out in the open she begged me not to give you a hard time! She insisted that you must have had good reason because you were too gentle and loving to have harboured a bad one.'

Four determined strides brought him to the bedside. His dark gaze glittering, he reached for her hands and drew her to her feet. 'You have not a single thing to worry about on that score. Now—' he dealt her backside a gentle slap— 'get dressed.'

Cesare had made his excuses and headed for the room set aside for his high-tech office as soon as they returned to the villa, closely followed by the arrival of his PA, a brisk young man, bristling with the efficiency his boss demanded.

Despite Cesare's assurances Milly had been full of trepidation as she'd taken herself to Filomena's room. Her deception had to be unforgiveable, didn't it? She felt slightly nauseous at her own uncharacteristic devious behaviour.

But the old lady's delight in seeing her, the warmth of her welcome, laid her anxieties to rest, as did Filomena's immediate and regally imperious demand to sit out on the terrace for a while so that they could enjoy the air and have the talk she'd been itching for ever since Cesare had informed her that she was Milly, her companion's twin sister.

An operation that was treated as a military manoeuvre, everyone from Stefano to the youngest housemaid being enlisted to move the wooden table and benches from the rose-shaded arbour at one side of the terrace to make room for a cushion-piled armchair, Rosa herself bringing up the rear with a tray loaded with chilled orange juice and little almond cakes.

'I was a little puzzled,' Filomena admitted with her beautiful smile as she sat like a queen on her throne as her staff melted away, 'as to how my companion had so changed in character! If I had had my wits about me I would have suspected something. Brittleness all gone, replaced with warmth and gentleness. More thoughtfulness. Your choice of reading matter too; Dickens as opposed to the sex and shopping sagas your sister was so fond of. Please—I'm not saying her company wasn't good for me. At that time it was. I had become bored with myself and being old! Cesare had become convinced I had a death wish! Jilly took me out of it with her amusing chatter, her liveliness and those flashes of charm that were most in evidence when my grandson was around. Sometimes, in my room at night, I could hear her laughing with him on the path outside my windows, and I thought—no matter. Yes—' she brought herself back to what she had been saying '—such charm. It could make you forgive almost anything.'

'Even theft?' Milly had to ask, feeling deep shame on her twin's behalf.

'Even that. She must have been desperate and I have much wealth. But,' she added with a flash of asperity, 'I wouldn't condone it as a career choice. Now—we talk of brighter things.'

Over dinner, the first meal Filomena hadn't taken from a tray since her accident, Milly, feeling cold inside because although Cesare had finally joined them he had barely acknowledged her presence, broached the subject of her friend's wedding.

'Cleo's really keen for me to be her bridesmaid. I'd hate to disappoint her. And I do need to vacate the flat.' She had given up all hope of Jilly ever bothering to try to contact home in the near future. While Cesare had been away she had phoned Cleo and her landlord and had given her contact number should her sister remember she had a family and try to get in touch. But so far nothing.

Her face glowed with sudden unconcealed pleasure. She would have no need of the flat. She and Cesare were to be married! The thought had the power to rock her, even though the way he'd been as good as ignoring her up until now had made her feel invisible!

'And when does this event take place?' Cesare had joined them at the last minute and it was the first she had seen of him since he'd shut himself away in his office.

She met the cool questioning of his eyes and a wave of intense disappointment surged through her. Last night those eyes had been filled with raw desire, sending her up in flames, now he was looking at her as if she were a menial asking for time off when it wasn't due to her!

'Around six weeks,' she answered unsteadily. 'But I'd need to go back to England a couple of weeks earlier. Dress fittings—that sort of thing. I'd come back the day after the wedding.'

His impressively handsome profile was turned to her now. He wasn't looking at her and Milly doubted that he had heard a word she'd said. It was left to Filomena to step into the breach.

'Then of course we must spare you. And who knows, you might learn something of your sister's whereabouts. From what you told me earlier, I know you worry about her complete disappearance. Cesare—' her voice sharpened '—you will arrange this?'

'Nonna—' He laid down his cutlery and leant back in his chair, an ebony brow elevated just slightly. 'If you recall, I will not be here to arrange anything. However—' he pushed back his chair and stood up in one fluid movement, the very image of cool Italian sophistication '—give Stefano the details and he will make the travel arrangements. Now, if you will excuse me, I still have work to do before I leave for Madrid in the morning.'

How Milly got through the rest the meal and

the ritual of helping Filomena get ready for bed while behaving as if she was perfectly happy she would never know.

Cesare had as good as looked through her, she fretted as she reached the sanctuary of her own bedroom. Had not addressed her except to ask that clipped question. It hurt quite unbearably. She was hard put to reconcile his attitude over dinner with that of the man who had made glorious love to her, had asked her to be his wife.

Deciding to get up extra early, run him to earth and demand a few answers before he left in the morning, she had a quick shower, brushed her teeth and climbed into bed wearing a baggy old T-shirt. She felt too emotional to creep through the silent house to his office and demand answers now. Right now. Her pride wouldn't let her show him how insecure she felt.

He hadn't once said he loved her, she reminded herself on a flood of nervy anxiety. Then told herself to grow up and swiftly assured herself that no man in his right mind would ask a woman to marry him, share his life and bear his children if he didn't love her and, anyway, he probably had a whole load of stuff on his mind to do with his up-and-coming extended business trip.

Too much stuff to give much thought to his fiancée when he would, with man-like pragmatism, consider enough had been said on the subject of what he felt for her to make emotional scenes and the display of female insecurities plain annoying. Make him think that she would prove to be a demanding wife, whining and complaining when he put business first, throwing a hissy-fit if he ever dared to be late home by as much as a single minute.

Reaching that sensible conclusion, she flicked off the bedside light and closed her eyes only to open them again almost immediately as the door opened and Cesare, wearing a towelling robe, was illuminated by the light from the broad passage behind before the door closed again and he was at the bedside breathing, 'Forgive me, *mi amore!*'

He reached for her in the darkness, pulling her into the circle of his arms. 'I ignored you!' he confessed rawly. 'I couldn't look at you, talk to you, without aching to have you in my arms, to kiss you! I need you so much I would have given our secret away. Nonna may be old but she's far from stupid!' He breathed in very deep, his lips against the side of her neck. 'Say you forgive me!'

'Anything! I forgive you anything!' Melting against him, Milly slid her hands beneath his robe, her fingers splaying against the hard, muscular planes of his chest, breathing in the aphrodisiacal scent of warm male and a slightly tangy aftershave, her head swimming dizzily on a wave of love and longing and annoyance with herself for feeling any insecurities whatsoever.

Immeasurably flattered because he'd admitted he couldn't look at her without betraying a primitive urge to make love to her,

her brain reeling with the knowledge of her feminine power, she lifted her head and put her soft mouth against his lips, very gently, and teased softly, 'Then I know what I must do to test your powers of endurance to the limit, don't I?'

'*Strega!* It is just as well I am to be away from the temptation of you while Nonna completes her recovery!' And then he claimed her mouth with a passionate intensity that made her heart beat wildly and somehow his robe got lost in the vortex and her T-shirt went the same way as his tongue mated with hers with driven hunger until he reared away, flicking on the bedside light.

'I need to look at you, *amore mia*. I need to feast my eyes,' he announced raggedly. He laid her back on the bed. 'I need to touch.' His voice thickened. 'Here—' Reverent fingers brushed her tight nipples and her breath caught in roughened gasps as those same fingers stroked over the flat planes of her tummy, then lower. 'And here—'

As his hand brushed through the golden curls at the apex of her thighs and discovered the aching, molten heat, excitement had her writhing against him, her every enticing movement begging him to take the burning ache for him away. As if he understood her uncontrollable hunger, he kissed her with such sweet tenderness she thought she might die from it and murmured softly, 'Slowly, *mi amore*. Tonight I will take you to Paradise many times, I promise you.'

CHAPTER TWELVE

IT WAS POURING with rain and the flat felt damp and chilly. Shorn of the curtains and rugs, the brightly coloured cushions she'd bought one cold winter day in an attempt to make their home look more cheerful, the place looked what it was, drab and dingy.

Milly's throat tightened at the thought that her mother, living in pleasant, leafy suburban comfort while her husband had been alive, had been reduced to this during her final years. And all because of Jilly's wildly selfish schemes.

Surveying the assembled packing cases, Milly felt a stab of deep sadness, they represented the sum total of her mother's life.

Pathetically little.

She'd packed the remainder of Jilly's possessions and had taken the more respectable items of hers and her mother's clothing to a charity shop and even now removal men were taking the packing cases and furniture into storage because at some time in the future Jilly might need some of it if she returned to set up home in England and she felt bad about disposing of everything without consulting Jilly first.

That was if her sister ever turned up!

She didn't know what she felt most, anger at her twin for her less than honest behaviour and her blithe disregard for her family, or deepening anxiety at her mysterious disappearance.

Whatever— She turned from the window and the unprepossesing view of the rain-soaked high street and the top of the removal van parked outside the butcher's shop and went to the poky apology for a kitchen to brew tea for the removal men. Fretting about her twin wouldn't solve anything.

At least yesterday, the day of Cleo's

wedding, had been warm and sunny. Her friend had looked beautiful and the groom proud enough to bust a gut, she recalled, determined to think of something cheerful.

Besides, she would be returning to Italy tomorrow after overnighting at an airport hotel and soon now, very soon, she would be seeing Cesare again.

Her spirits soared. She'd missed him so much, but soon the waiting would be over. After his departure, in the weeks before she'd returned to England, he'd phoned the villa twice a week to speak to his grandmother and ask after her state of health and on a couple of occasions she'd been able to speak to him herself and those conversations had been heartwarmingly precious.

She poured tea into mugs and set them on a tray. Cesare had even gone to the trouble of setting up a credit account for her use, which was really generous of him because they weren't yet married. She was merely his secret fiancée, though she'd been hard put to keep quiet, especially as Cleo had done a lot of probing over what she called the 'blackmailing Italian guy.'

She'd longed to state that he was completely wonderful and soon to be her husband. Only her promise to Cesare to keep their plans secret had kept her from confiding her wonderful news.

But Filomena was now as good as new. Or so the old lady had affirmed when Milly phoned her a couple of days ago. Already she was directing a major overhaul of the long herbaceous border and was anxious for Milly's return and her horticultural input. So that meant there would be no further delay on Cesare divulging their wedding plans!

Her stomach flipped with electrifying excitement. He was all she could ever want and then some. And he wanted to marry her!

Leaning against the chipped enamel draining board, misty-eyed and moony at that world-shaking prospect, the tea forgotten, the shouts and grunts of the three men who were humping the ancient sofa down the narrow staircase receding, her imagination conjured up a blissful image of her wedding day, her fabulous dress—all white and floaty, or maybe satin and sleek—the clearest image of all that of Cesare looking stunningly fantastic, his dark head turned, his eyes drenched with love as she walked towards him up the aisle—

'Milly!'

She tensed, breath locked in her lungs, hazy romantic images dispelled by something so immediate and real it set her heart racing.

Only one man made her plain ordinary name sound special. Only one man's voice could send shivers of delight skittering down her spine.

Cesare!

Galvanised, she fled from the kitchen and hurtled down the wooden staircase, erupting into his open arms with a squeal of welcoming delight. The sound was stopped right there in her throat as he lowered his dark head and kissed her with a ravishing thoroughness that left her feeling helplessly dizzy.

'I needed that, *cara,*' he at last announced with husky conviction, holding her by her upper arms so that he could look at her properly.

'*Bella, bella.* Perfection!' Lushly veiled eyes drifted over the elegant pale lemon-coloured linen suit she had chosen to travel in with its waist clipping jacket and narrow knee-length skirt. 'You choose well when not constrained by near poverty,' he approved, his eyes homing in on the swell of her breasts hinted at by the classy cut of the jacket.

Milly squirmed, her lovely face flushing uncomfortably. She so didn't want him to think she was greedy, out for all she could get!

But this suit had cost an arm and a leg and, dithering over it, severely tempted, Cleo had dealt the knockout blow. 'You must have it. It's perfect for you!' And the amount of credit on the card Cesare had set up for her was mind boggling.

'Cleo and I had a day in London before the wedding,' she confessed. 'I had my hair done.' And that had cost a small fortune, she recalled, her blush reviving with a vengeance as she relived the guilt that had swamped her when she'd seen the size of the bill.

In the past she had slipped out in her lunch hour and Marjorie in the salon just up the road had cut it for her for a minute fraction of the cost. But she had to admit that the London guy had done a much better job.

'And I bought a few things. Not too many, I promise,' she ended on an uncomfortable whisper.

'*Amore mia*—' He dropped a kiss on her luscious mouth. 'What is mine is yours.' He smiled into her wide emerald eyes. 'As my wife you will have the best. I expect it. No, I demand it,' he stated firmly, moving her aside as one of the removal men clattered down the stairs with the rolled up rug that had softened the bare boards of the tiny bedroom set aside for Jilly's use.

'We found the tea, luv!' He gave her a broad wink and Cesare enquired, 'How much longer?'

'Just finishing, guv.'

Cesare glanced at the slim gold watch that banded his flat wrist. 'Five minutes, tops.'

Receiving an assurance, he turned his attention to Milly. 'Ready to leave?'

'I've just got to fetch my case.' A new one to hold the lovely things she'd bought. She felt her cheeks turn pink again and hurriedly informed herself that he seemed fine about her spending some of his money, so she really had nothing to feel guilty about. One day soon she was going to have to make him understand that his wealth meant nothing to her. She'd marry him if he was a pauper and she'd happily go out scrubbing floors to put bread on the table!

Mounting the stairs at a rush, she wondered what the hurry meant. That he couldn't wait to be alone with her? Her heart beat faster. In one of his recent phone calls to his grandmother he had probably heard that today she would be packing up and leaving the flat and had dropped everything to be with her.

Wondering if he could get a seat on her flight back to Italy tomorrow, she decided that his all-fired rush to get out of here at least meant she didn't have the time to get maudlin over the sad memories she was leaving behind. That was all to the good since she had such a blissful future to look forward to.

He took the case from her the moment her feet touched the bottom stair and, while she was locking the outer door and posting the key back through the letter box for the landlord to collect, she smiled up at him through the drizzle. 'I didn't expect you. I'm so glad you came.'

'Nonna told me you were due back at Pisa Airport tomorrow. I cut into my itinerary and took the chance that you would still be here. There is a chauffeured limo waiting to take us to the airport. The company jet's ready to fly us south.'

'My! You certainly know how to whisk a girl off her feet!' She grinned up at him, feeling immensely privileged and proud to be about to be married to a guy who only had to click his fingers to have his needs of the moment catered to immediately. The sort of guy whose personal magnetism made him stand head and shoulders above the rest, regardless of wealth and standing.

He didn't return her smile. His classically gorgeous features were stamped in stern mould and, shaken, she voiced a sudden fear. 'Is anything wrong? Filomena?'

'Nonna is fine.' He hooked an arm around her shoulders and began pacing towards a sleek silver limo. 'Your sister has finally been located. Working in Naples. I am here to take you to her.'

'I don't see why I shouldn't go to her now,' Milly stated as Cesare emerged from the *en suite* bathroom, rubbing his hair with a towel. She turned from watching the brilliant sunset from the enormous soundproof windows of the luxurious modern hotel room he had brought her to, explaining that although there were older, more atmospheric places he could have chosen, Naples was a noisy city and such raucous bombardment of their auditory senses would not be conducive to a decent night's rest, adding with a slashing grin that made her heart flip that a decent night's rest wasn't his top priority.

'The morning would be best.' He tossed the towel aside.

Milly sighed. He looked heartbreakingly gorgeous with his damp dark hair mussed, his impressive torso delineated by a black T-shirt that topped beautifully cut stone-coloured chinos. She quelled the immediate urge to go to him, snuggle up, forget everything else. She had an entirely valid point to make.

'She'll be at work in the morning.'

'She's working now.' He paced to her, rubbed a light fingertip over the frown line between her eyes. 'Your sister now rejoices in the name of Jacinta Le Bouchard and works as an exotic dancer and hostess in the type of nightclub I wouldn't expect or want you to go near.'

Milly felt her spine crumple. The hostess bit was obviously a euphemism, judging by the way his mouth had flattened with distaste. Surely her poor sister hadn't been reduced to selling her body to any man willing to hand over a fistful of money?

No wonder that during the flight over he had said little more on the subject other than that his investigator had tracked Jilly down to Naples, reiterating his promise that she would have time alone with her twin initially in order to break the news of the loss of their mother but that he would then give her the lecture of her life, although he did not intend to press charges of theft.

'I'm sorry, *amore mia*.' He folded gentle arms around her and splayed his fingers in her silky blonde hair as he drew her head against his heart. 'If I could have spared you any of this I would have done. You are naturally worried for her future welfare,' he soothed. 'And for your sake I promise to find her more salubrious employment, provided she agrees that her lifestyle must change.'

He held her a little away from his body, 'And now I suggest you shower and change. I'll order from room service and we will have a night of such pleasure that you will forget your anxieties over tomorrow. Yes?'

His dark eyes were brimming with tenderness and her love for him overflowed, making it difficult to breathe. He was such an intrinsically good man. She adored him so much it hurt!

For her sake he was willing to put his previously driven need to see Jilly clapped in irons behind him, even to the extent of offering her a way out of the present seemingly dodgy career she had embarked upon. So for his sake she would put her twin right out of her head. Tomorrow morning would come soon enough.

'I love you,' she breathed, distinctly disinclined to part from him even for the space of time she would need to take a swift shower and gained herself a fleeting kiss, a mere butterfly brush of his lips against hers and a husky command to, 'Go now. Before you wreck my plans for a night to remember!'

And, as she headed for the sumptuous bedroom and the luxurious *en suite* bathroom, the blood fizzing in her veins over that promise of a night to remember, he called softly, 'Don't spend ages dressing up for me, *cara*. I am not a patient man!'

Patience was a virtue in short supply as Milly showered in record time and, not even bothering to slip into the complimentary bathrobe, sped to the bedroom to fling open her suitcase. As her fingers encountered cool silk a Mona Lisa smile curved her full lips.

Perfect!

The black silk nightie she'd been completely unable to resist when she'd laid eyes on it in a stylish London boutique had been earmarked for their wedding night. But what the heck! There was nothing to stop her wearing it for him now!

It was an impractical confection of whispering sheer silk that had had Cleo breathing, 'Wow! Sinful, or what? Sure there isn't a man in your life—and I don't mean the stodgy Bruce either?'

Explosive heat erupted deep in her pelvis as she slipped into it, her breasts tingling as they peaked against the cool fabric and her tummy fluttered as she encountered her image in one of the full length mirrors.

The silk clung everywhere. It subtly moulded every last intimate contour of her body, only the just-above-the-knee length side split allowing the wearer to walk.

The words brazen and siren slipped into her mind so she roughly pushed them out again. Cesare was her future husband.

But he'd said that he'd found Jilly's in-your-face-sexy choice of apparel to be a total turn-off.

Diving back into her suitcase she pulled out the matching negligee and slipped it on and if she still looked too come-and-grab-me she'd just have to start over, dig out a dress and fresh underwear.

An agitated appraisal did something to settle her nerves. Dressing like a vamp didn't come naturally to her—hadn't she loathed wearing her twin's cast-offs? The negligee helped. Sleeveless too, it was generously cut, falling in graceful folds to her ankles, the edges banded with delicate silk ruffles.

A little sigh of relief quivered on her soft mouth. Better. And anyway, what was wrong with a woman looking willing when she was about to spend the night with her soon-to-be husband?

On a wave of renewed confidence she opened the door to the living area. Cesare was standing at the huge window looking down at the teeming city, his hands thrust deep into the pockets of his chinos. He looked so commanding, so gorgeous that she just stopped breathing. And as she swayed towards him—it was the only form of locomotion she could manage because of the tight cut of the nightie—he turned and watched her, a smile of all-male appreciation wreathing his stunning features.

'Gift wrapped too!' He strode forward to meet her necessarily slinky approach, taking both her hands, holding her a little away from him, and his gleaming dark eyes swept slowly over her from head to toe with hot appreciation, making her cheeks glow and her heart beat like a steam hammer.

Lean hands slid to her slender waist, tugging her closer to the hard perfection of his body. 'I just lost my appetite for food,' he confided in a husky undertone. His lips found her earlobe. 'However, we will both make an effort.' His mouth moved to the sensitive hollow beneath her jaw and Milly's knees immediately turned to water. 'Anticipation adds spice, don't you think?'

His accent had never been so pronounced Milly decided, completely intoxicated by him as he led her to the alcove where a low table fronted a voguish deeply upholstered sofa.

White linen napkins, heavy silver flatware, elegant crystal glasses, champagne on ice and a mouthwatering array of seafood, salad and pasta dishes. Milly couldn't imagine eating any of it, she thought as she slid on to the sofa. Sexual tension was closing her throat up. Impossible to swallow the smallest morsel.

But when Cesare handed her a glass of the foaming liquid and angled his lean muscular body on to the sofa beside her she relaxed just a little until his knee touched hers and sheet lightning shot from that heated spot right into the private pulsating heart of her.

Her need for him was driving her crazy! Shakily, she put the glass down on the table just as Cesare angled his hips to extract a small velvet-covered box from a side pocket.

He put it into her nerveless fingers. 'For you, *amore mia*. Open it.'

For a long moment her eyes meshed with his. He had never said he loved her, but his eyes said it for him. Her heart full to bursting point, she lifted the lid. And gasped.

The square cut emerald in its simple gold setting was spectacular. Tanned lean fingers extracted the ring from its velvet nest and slipped it on her finger.

'For me!' Eyes as deeply green as the magnificent stone lifted to him, watched his mouth curve.

'I don't recall asking anyone else to marry me. And this…' He took a fine gold chain she'd been too dazzled by the emerald to notice from the velvet box and dangled it from his fingers. 'With this you can wear my ring around your neck until we are together to tell Nonna of our wedding plans, when she is stronger. But wear it now, wear it for me.'

Still too dazzled by the brilliance of the exquisite gem to grasp his meaning, she tipped her head on one side. 'I don't understand. We'll both be returning to the villa after—after tomorrow, won't we?'

'Alas, no. As I said, I broke into my itinerary to bring you here. Tomorrow afternoon you will fly to Pisa, where Stefano will meet you. And I go to London for a series of crucial meetings with the CEO of the fine gems offshoot and the top two designers.'

Disappointment hit Milly hard. She had so hoped—believed—that they would return together to break the wonderful news to Filomena, begin to organise their wedding.

Thankfully, common sense came to her rescue and stopped her whining like a child deprived of a favourite toy. Cesare had a huge world-spanning business empire to run and he was the sort of guy who firmly believed in the hands-on approach. And of course Filomena needed to get her strength back before she threw herself into wedding plans, as Cesare had warned she would.

She lifted her glass and raised it to him, her eyes glinting with teasing laughter now she'd got her priorities straightened out. 'To the longest secret engagement on record!'

'Not that long, I promise.' His response was

sombre, and she didn't quite know what to read into that change of mood, then thought nothing more of it when he selected a fork and began to feed her delicious morsels. Reciprocating, she fed him and the mood was good again. Close. Warm. Until, reaching forward to spear a yummy-looking piece of lobster for him she noted that the edges of her robe had parted, displaying full breasts lovingly moulded by wispy black silk, and noticed with a shock of pleasure that his eyes were riveted.

Laying down the fork he'd been using, he muttered in his own language, something that she took to be an imprecation, rose to his feet and scooped her into his arms with a husky, 'There's only so much anticipation a guy can take!' and carried her into the bedroom.

Even through the tinted glass windows Milly could see that the narrow streets they were driving through at a snail's pace looked pretty sleazy. For the first time this morning she was beginning to feel edgy about the coming encounter with her sister.

She'd woken feeling fabulous, sated and limp limbed from what had truly turned out to be a night to remember. Cesare had brought her breakfast on a tray. Juice, coffee, toast and thin slices of ham.

He'd joined her, easing his lean boxer-clad body beside her, and in no time at all he'd reached out and smoothed a hand over the curve of her naked shoulder, drawing her to him murmuring unsteadily, 'You're so sexy. I can't keep my hands off you.'

'I don't want you to,' she'd confessed huskily, drowning in pleasure as his fingers caressed her distended nipples. Pushing the tray aside, she'd turned then, her body stretching out to connect with his. With uninhibited passion she had hooked her fingers around the waistband of his boxer shorts and pulled them down.

And the rest, as they said, was history!

Later they'd showered together with predictable results. Her body glowed at the memory.

She'd still been on cloud nine while she'd dressed in the cream-coloured linen trousers and a tailored dark green cool cotton shirt while Cesare had gone to the lounge area. She'd heard him talking on his mobile, first in English and then in his own language with no room in her head for a single thought that centred on her delinquent twin.

Now as the driver negotiated the tangled warren of streets, the thought of the coming difficult interview made her heart thump and her stomach turn over. As if attuned to her every thoughtwave, Cesare's fingers tightened around hers as he stated, 'There's nothing to worry about, *cara*. Don't let her browbeat you or spin a tissue of lies. Simply break the news about your mother, tell her I have incontrovertible proof that she stole from my grandmother and leave the rest to me. I promise I won't involve the police.'

On an impulse she rested her head against

his broad shoulder. 'I'm grateful. I know she deserves to have the book thrown at her, but—'

'She is your twin sister and there is a bond,' he finished for her. 'I can understand. Though I strongly doubt she would feel the same.' And before she could argue with that, remind him that Jilly had always looked out for her when they'd been kids Cesare announced, 'We seem to have arrived.'

They were parked in front of firmly closed doors with peeling paintwork flanked by grimy glass fronted panels containing coloured photographs of scantily clad females in suggestive poses. Inexpertly painted names were angled over and beneath them. Jacinta Le Bouchard prominent among them.

Feeling decidedly anxious over her twin's disastrous career choice, not to mention her even dodgier future prospects, as Cesare helped her out of the sleek black car she watched as he leaned in the front and spoke to the driver, who nodded, picked a newspaper from the front seat and settled down to read.

'Come.' He cupped a hand beneath her elbow as they entered a narrow malodorous alley beside the nightclub. 'I will leave you alone with her for twenty minutes, half an hour max, before I join you. When that is over the driver will take us to the airport and I will see you on a flight to Pisa before heading for London,' he told her flatly, releasing her elbow, some kind of tension hardening the sculpted angles of his stunning profile.

He was making her too uneasy to say anything more than a mumbled, 'Thanks.'

She felt suddenly that a great yawning gulf had opened up between them, that he was deliberately distancing himself from her. Had coming face to face with the way her twin was earning a living given him second thoughts about having anything to do with her, let alone marrying her and introducing tainted blood into his high status family?

The thought was unworthy, too horrible to contemplate. Milly ousted it with a decisive shake of her head and followed him up a short flight of crumbling stone steps, through an open doorway and into a narrow passage.

The first door he came to—more flaking paintwork—bore a card with the cringe-making 'Jacinta Le Bouchard' printed on it in violet ink. Pressing his finger on the bell, keeping it there, his jaw set, he didn't look at her. His mouth was flat with contemptuous distaste when, after a minute or two, the door was roughly dragged open and Jilly stood there, wearing a kimono splashed all over with brightly coloured dragons, her long hair all over the place, her mouth dropping open with shock.

Turning, he levelled an unreadable look at her and Milly paled, even more colour leaving her face as he turned on his heel and strode back down the narrow passage as if he couldn't wait to get away. Her troubled eyes followed him every step of the way until he disappeared out of sight.

Was he recalling her initial deception, lumping her morals with her twin's? Two of a kind?

'What the hell are you doing here with that bastard?'

Milly turned to face her twin. Her unwelcoming face still bore traces of last night's make-up and it wasn't like Jilly to be less than ultra-fastidious about her skin care routine, she thought with a pang, making herself remember that she was here for a purpose. 'Can I come in?'

As a reply Jilly turned and walked across the tiny hallway and through a beaded curtain. Milly followed, leaving the front door open, because who knew when she'd leave her twin to her own devices and leg it after Cesare to make him explain why he'd looked at her as if she was the last person on earth he wanted to be with?

Gathering herself with the reminder that there were things that had to be said, she brushed through the hanging strands of beads and stepped into a room which one look told her served as sitting room, bedroom and kitchen. Clothes were strewn everywhere and Milly had the unfond memory of how, for as far as her memory stretched back she'd had to clear up after her twin.

'I'm afraid I've got bad news,' she said softly as her twin parked herself on the scarlet satin covered bed.

'Spit it out then.' With an uninterested shrug, Jilly reached for a pack of cigarettes and lit up, blowing a plume of smoke towards the ceiling.

Milly moved closer, ready to offer comfort. There was no way to break this gently. 'I'm sorry, but Ma passed away a few months ago. It was sudden.' She reached for her twin's cigarette free hand, noted the sudden frown between the mirror-image of her own eyes, and could have wept for her, vividly remembering her own shock and grief. 'I would have contacted you,' she impressed on her quietly, 'but I didn't know how. You hadn't been in touch since you left Florence.'

Jilly's face went pale and still, her jaw clenched, as if she were desperately holding back strong emotion. Shock and grief, Milly thought on a pang of painful sympathy, her fingers tightening around her twins.'

Jilly dragged her hand away. 'Then how did you find me? How did you meet up with that bastard?' Her mouth twisted as she stubbed the cigarette out in an overflowing ashtray.

Milly, stunned, threw at her, 'Is that all you can say? Don't you feel anything? Don't you care?' She took a pace back. The sister she'd admired and loved all her life now seemed like a stranger.

Jilly shrugged. 'It's a lot to take in. 'Course I care, damn you! So don't come the Holy Joe with me! Anyway, she didn't have much to live for, did she?'

'And whose fault was that?' Milly wanted to strangle her! 'At least she died firmly believing you'd one day make good the money you lost. She kept faith.'

'Well, I did try,' Jilly defended herself, for

the first time looking uncomfortable, and Milly tipped a pile of underwear off a chair and sat down because her legs had started to shake beneath her. She had never said a harsh word to her twin in her life and now she couldn't seem to stop.

'How?' she demanded, tight lipped. 'By stealing it?'

'What did you say?' Jilly looked as though sibling strangling was a two way street.

Taking a deep breath, Milly told herself that they were getting nowhere by yelling at each other. As calmly as she could, she ran through the whole story, starting at the point where Cesare had mistaken her for Jilly and she had gone along with it, getting so caught up in the plot that she ended with, 'He's been really good about it. Those cheques you forged, I mean. He's got the proof but he promised not to take it any further.' Her eyes sparkled with tears. 'Oh, Jilly—how could you do that? I'm really worried for you!'

'The bastard's got you well and truly hooked!'

'What are you talking about?' Milly looked into her twin's eyes and shivered. Cold. Hard. Two flags of bright colour flamed angrily on her cheekbones.

'I think you know. Or if you don't you're even dafter than I thought you were!' Jilly took another cigarette, the wreathing plume of smoke making her eyes look mean and narrow. 'Is that his ring you're wearing? Has he got you into bed yet?' Taking the violent flush that suffused her twin's face as an affirmative, seeing the way she instinctively placed a protective hand over the huge emerald, she snapped. 'I thought so. So cut the lecturing. Okay, so I helped myself to some of the old girl's money. It's not as if she'd miss it; the old bat's loaded.' Shooting off the bed, she paced the cluttered room then swung round, faced Milly and announced bitterly, 'And after Cesare dumped me when I told him I was expecting his baby, I needed it!'

CHAPTER THIRTEEN

MILLY FELT THE blood drain from her face as wave after wave of dizziness made her sway where she sat. She clutched at the sides of the chair for support. This wasn't happening. It could not be happening! She must have misheard.

'You're expecting Cesare's child?' Her voice sounded weak, threadlike, her eyes pleading, begging to hear a denial.

'Was,' Jilly corrected with a sigh. 'I miscarried. I had a tough time with the early stages of the pregnancy—it was the reason I didn't come home to England. Ma would have been devastated with the shame of having a daughter who had a baby without the benefit of a wedding ring on her finger—you know what she was like.'

Milly put her fingertips to her temples. The squalid room was tilting around her and her ears were buzzing. She had known this interview would be difficult. But not as bad as this, please, not as bad as this!

She flinched as Jilly put a hand on her shoulder, shaking her head violently as her twin asked, 'Want a brandy or something, kid?'

Rebellion stirred. She wasn't a kid! And Cesare wasn't the type of man to turn his back on his own child. He was her future husband! She trusted him, didn't she?

It was on the tip of her tongue to tell Jilly that she knew she had to be lying because Cesare had confessed that he found Jilly a total turn-off but, to spare her sister's feelings, she kept her mouth shut. It would be bad enough for her to know she'd been branded a thief without the further humiliation of hearing that the gorgeous Cesare Saracino preferred the quieter twin over the sex-on-legs version.

'We're going to be married, I won't believe

anything bad of him!' The words were out before she could stop them.

She cringed when her twin countered drily, 'Yeah? 'Course you are. That's what he led me to believe too.'

Jilly dragged a chair from under the table and settled at Milly's side. 'Listen kid, you're in denial and I can't blame you. But haven't I always looked out for you?'

'Like you did when you left me to pick up the pieces after you lost every penny Ma had and more? Not that I minded looking after her the best I could, but you could at least have phoned or written, told us where you were and what you were doing.' Attack was the best form of defence, wasn't it? Anything to change the subject, because she couldn't bear to hear any more of Jilly's lies. They were lies, weren't they? They had to be! She tried to stand, to leave this hateful place, but her legs had turned to jelly and wouldn't hold her upright. Miserably she sank back on the chair and let her twin's words wash over her.

'I had my reasons, okay? Listen, there I was working in an upmarket club in Florence when this fabulous guy walks in with another man. Every woman around was riveted. Well, he's pretty hard to overlook. I think I fell for him there and then. I asked around and found he was the head of the Saracino empire. Next thing I knew he was advertising for a companion for his ancient grandmother. I was in there like a shot, and he hired me on the spot. I could tell he was interested. Well a girl can, can't she? Well, things progressed. From what I gathered from the old woman, he was rarely home—flying here, there and everywhere on business—but he hung around because of me. And, give him his due, he's a fantastic lover. Talk about insatiable! He vowed he loved me, all the usual guff, asked me to marry him.' She snorted her contempt. 'Even gave me a ring.'

Picking up Milly's hand, she examined the emerald, her eyes narrowing with spite. 'Yeah. Same one. I left it behind. I would have kept it and sold it and not had to dip my fingers into the old bat's bank account out of desperation. But I had it valued. It's a cheap fake. Like him! 'Course, I wasn't supposed to wear it openly,' she scorned. 'He wanted to bring the old woman round slowly to the idea of his marrying a foreigner.'

Her jaw set, as if she were trying to keep emotion at bay. 'If you still don't believe me you could tackle him head on. He'll deny it, of course. And if you ask the old woman for corroboration of the so-called engagement you'll draw a blank. He made sure she knew nothing about it. And I fell for it. I was madly in love with him and believed every lying word he said. I even thought with him being so filthy rich he would give me a whopping allowance after we were married and I could begin to pay Ma back. But face it, kid, his kind doesn't marry down. When he proposes and actually means it she'll be upper crust and filthy rich.'

Milly stared at her twin with shattered eyes

as the words dripped agonisingly into her mind like poison. She didn't want to believe any of this but—

Had Cesare given her twin a chain too? To keep their fake engagement secret? He'd insisted that they keep their plans secret, hadn't he? Using his grandmother as an excuse, the same excuse he'd given Jilly. In her twin's case to give him time to talk the old lady round; in her own case he'd insisted that they wait to break the news until his grandmother was strong again.

It came to the same thing.

And why on earth would Jilly lie about the pregnancy? It made no kind of sense, she thought on a wave of nausea. Such a wicked fabrication would gain her absolutely nothing. It made far more sense to take everything she'd said as the truth.

Pregnant and dumped by the man she'd believed she would marry, she'd admitted she'd been desperate. And so she'd stolen what she'd thought she was owed. It didn't excuse theft, nothing ever would, but it did explain it.

A wave of dizziness attacked her and Jilly's voice came as if from far away, at the end of a long, echoing tunnel. 'Listen kid. Take my advice and dump him before he dumps you. Salvage some pride, get out before he comes back—if he ever does. Go back home, where you belong. Look.' She shot to her feet and crossed the room to pull a bundle of notes from beneath the scarlet-covered pillow. 'I'll even lend you the money for your fare back and call a cab to get you to the airport. So don't say I don't look out for you!'

Milly shook her head and forced herself to her feet, ignoring the proffered notes. Dragging in a deep breath, she straightened her slender shoulders. 'We're twins. Part of each other,' she stressed, her lips feeling as if they had been carved out of wood. 'Neither of us would knowingly do anything to harm the other. So do you swear that what you've said is the truth?'

'You really doubt me?' Green eyes rolled in

expressive disbelief. 'Would I have told you all that stuff if it wasn't gospel, when it shows me up as a gullible idiot? Look, Milly…' She attempted a hug but Milly stepped back, too close to breaking down to allow a sympathetic gesture that would have her falling to pieces. 'Take my advice, get out before he makes a fool of you too.'

Milly turned, her spine ramrod stiff. Cesare had said he'd give her time alone with her twin. But would he still be waiting in the car knowing that Jilly would surely spill the beans? Or would he have instructed the driver to take off, leaving her stranded?

As she entered the narrow hallway she decided bleakly that she hoped he had taken off. Being stranded in a strange city surrounded by people who didn't speak her language seemed preferable to seeing his handsome, devious, cruel face again.

The shock that had left her weak and shaky was replaced by searing anger. If she saw him again she would kill him! Beat him to a pulp just as he had taken her loving heart and ground it beneath his heels!

Blinded by rage, fuelled by a hurt that filled every inch of her with indescribable pain, she stepped out on to the hot pavement and collided with a wall of stunning Italian manhood.

Too stunning by half! Feeling those strong arms go round her, she pushed him away and, all dignity deserting her, she lifted her chin in wounded defiance and held his dark as night, devious eyes, dragged his ring off her finger, dropped it and yelled brokenly, 'Put it back in the Christmas cracker!'

'*Cara*—' He reached for her but she leapt back, her voice choky as she informed him of her opinion of his character. 'Don't touch me, you—you despicable louse! I never want to see you again!'

And no way would she share that car with him! She'd find her own way back to the hotel on foot to collect her stuff, even if it took the rest of the day! She knew a brief flare of triumph as a youth on a skateboard bore down on the gap between them blocking Cesare's way. She took the opportunity to scramble into the waiting car, not understanding the rapid flow of Italian Cesare directed at the driver, not caring either. She gabbled, 'Back to the hotel, pronto!' hoping the driver understood and more desperately hoping that Cesare wouldn't climb in after her, then sank in a heap of misery against the leather upholstery as the car drew away and Cesare turned abruptly and entered her twin's lodging place, his stride ominous, his shoulders rigid.

Stifling the urge to give way to wildly abandoned weeping kept her fully occupied as the car made its stately progress through the narrow streets and she was unsurprised when she was deposited outside the hotel they had used, where their luggage was waiting to be collected. The louse would have instructed the driver to bring her back here to collect her belongings then leave her, she realised, fuming, barely heeding the driver's thickly accented, 'You to wait. *Capice?*' before, as predicted, he drove away, leaving her to find her own way back to England. Which was no punishment, she thought savagely, because that was precisely what she meant to do!

Her small face grim, she swept into the main reception area, adamantly dismissing the driver's instructions to wait. What for? To hang around like a spare part that had no further use, just for the privilege of seeing the wretch one last time when he finally appeared to collect his own luggage. Not likely!

Thankfully, the chief receptionist spoke fluent English and was obliging enough to call a cab to take her to the airport, exchanging the small reserve of sterling in her purse for euros to enable her to pay the fare. Unfortunately, she would have to use her credit card to buy a ticket back to the UK. She would be in debt, jobless and homeless. But those problems were small change compared with the devastating pain of a shattered heart and savaged dreams, she thought wretchedly as she paid off the driver and made her way into the departures hall, hardly having the mental energy left to wonder if there would be a spare seat on the next flight back home which, so the obliging receptionist had informed her, was scheduled to leave in half an hour from now.

Cesare exited the hotel at speed and hurled himself back into the waiting chauffeur driven car and in moments they were heading for the airport.

She hadn't waited. His jaw tightened. Had he expected her to? After the admissions he'd dragged from her twin, he acknowledged bitterly that waiting for him would be the last thing she could stomach.

The seven kilometre drive to the airport seemed to be taking for ever. Venting a savage expletive he leant forward to instruct the driver to break all speed records. According to the receptionist, the *signorina* was hoping to get a flight back to London. And that flight would be leaving in fifteen minutes!

He ground his strong white teeth in desperate frustration then subsided in black anxiety. Even if by some miracle the flight had been delayed and he caught up with her would he ever be able to regain her trust after what her sister had told her? By some unholy coincidence her lies would have struck a chord, ringing true to Milly. Even back when Nonna had insisted on hiring her, his instinct had told him that Jilly Lee was bad news. She was a thief, a liar, a self-centred taker. Her twin was a giver, a life enhancer. And he loved her more than life. His gut twisted.

He glanced at his watch and fisted his hands at his sides. They'd arrived at the airport environs just as her flight was taking off.

Frustration roared through him but, never one to give up, Cesare was already deciding his next course of action. His private jet was scheduled to take off for London in an hour. He wouldn't be that far behind her. He had no means of knowing where she would go now that she'd vacated the flat. But he'd track down the friend whose wedding she'd attended and, through her, find the love of his life.

Simultaneously Cesare and the driver saw her. A slight figure standing outside the departures area. Cesare sent up a silent prayer of gratitude as the car slid to a rubber-burning halt.

She looked lost. He exited the car at speed, something twisting inside him as his eyes took in her lone, forlorn figure. His heart was bursting with a deep, protective love. He strode towards her, his heart thumping heavily in the cavity of his chest. Paces away, she lifted her bright head and he could swear he saw relief spark in the depths of her lovely sea-green eyes.

He wanted to fold his arms around her, hold her, never let her go. But the situation was too delicate for that. Regaining her trust was his absolute priority.

Her slight shoulders straightened. 'I didn't know if I would be able to find you.' Relief flooded her voice. 'By the time I got back to the hotel you might have already left.'

'But I would have found you, *cara mia*. I would have searched the whole world for you.'

Milly searched his eyes, the force field of strong emotion emanating from him holding her spellbound. Her voice shook as she confided, 'I meant to try to get back to England. But I just stood there like a prune because it hit me that if what Jilly said had been true you wouldn't even have told me she'd been found, never mind taking me there and giving me time alone with her because you would have known she would tell me— things.' A flush of colour stole over her ashen cheeks.

Controlling the driven impetus to take her in his arms, rain kisses on her heartbreakingly lovely face, took some doing but he was rewarded when she stated with distress, 'I threw your beautiful ring back at you, called you names. I—I lost faith. I didn't even bother to ask you if what she'd told me was true— about you promising to marry her then ditching her when she told you she was carrying your child. I believed her as I always have. I'm so sorry.'

Her head bowed on the slender stalk of her neck and Cesare snatched in a deep ragged breath and gathered her in his arms regardless of interested onlookers who, being Italian, would probably start applauding any time now.

'*Per amor di Dio!* You believe in me now; that is all that matters,' he murmured, his lips tantalisingly close to hers now. 'I made your sister admit to the lies she had told and I must admit that for a moment I was furious that you hadn't trusted me over her! But my fabled common sense kicked in.' A finger beneath her chin had her downcast eyes meeting his wry grin. 'And it told me that her lies would have sounded convincing and that some-where, away from me, you were feeling in shock, betrayed and hurting. It was unbear-able for me!' he claimed extravagantly. 'And I swear on my life and on yours that I never so much as touched your wretched sister! But

I think you have worked that out for yourself. That I want you to be my wife, that I truly love you, more than any words of mine can ever portray. Yes?'

'Yes!' Milly's heart swelled with love, so much love she could barely contain it. Her hands rose, her fingers tangling in the soft dark hair at the nape of his neck and he brought his mouth down on hers with a passion that scorched her soul. She loved him so much and she had almost lost him.

Immersed in emotion, it was long minutes later that Cesare raised his proud head and Milly saw through a daze of glorious happiness that they had gained an avid audience and she blushed to the roots of her hair as her stunningly handsome future husband gave the throng a wide grin then folded an arm around her shoulders and drew her to the waiting car, leaving the driver to retrieve her abandoned luggage.

A rapid string of instructions issued from lips that still echoed that grin. The moment the driver was behind the wheel and as the car was put in motion Cesare was already extracting a slim mobile from an inner pocket, speaking rapidly in Italian, his free hand clasping hers possessively. The moment he finished she asked, 'Are we both going to London?'

'Change of plan. My pilot is now getting ready to fly us to Florence. We are going home to break our news to Nonna. And if I have to tie her down to stop her from launching into wedding arrangements, then I will! My PA will handle my London meeting. From now on, where you are I will be during all the days of our wonderful future together.' His arm hooked around her shoulder, drawing her closer and she snuggled into him as he explained, 'Over the past few weeks I have been away from you and every moment was a torment. But it was a necessary evil if I was to make sure that everything was in place, making sure the more-than-able heads of the various enterprises knew of my plans.'

'Plans?' she murmured, her eyes limpid as

he placed a tantalising kiss on the corner of her mouth.

'To be with you. To spend the majority of my time with you and any future family we might have.' This time the kiss was full-blown and so spectacular that Milly was totally disorientated when they reached the private airstrip where the company jet was waiting.

Immediately after take-off Cesare reached for her hand and slipped the emerald back where it belonged, saying huskily, 'It would be a shame to put it into a Christmas cracker! I much prefer to see it on your finger.'

Blushing over the cheap jibe she'd thrown at him, she was further mortified when he lifted her hand to his lips and tenderly kissed each fingertip in turn and pronounced, 'It is a family heirloom, one of many. I will delight in seeing you shine in glittering diamonds, rubies as red as wine and more emeralds than you can possibly imagine.'

She wriggled in her seat as it really hit her that he must be one of the wealthiest men in

Christendom. She faced him squarely and told him staunchly, 'I only want you.'

'You have me. Body, heart and soul.' He settled her back into the curve of his arm. 'But a little extra won't come amiss, *mi amore*. And, talking of extras, I made a few phone calls this morning back at the hotel while you were dressing. I have arranged for your sister to take up a vacant receptionist's post in the New York Saracino complex. My agent will contact her with flight tickets and further instructions. And, before you get one tiny doubt about why I should be so magnanimous when she deserves to be damned to hell, I did this for you, not for her. I knew you would be happier, with a little long-distance help she could make a more hopeful future for herself, away from that seedy place. I know you care for her and would worry about her—and, more than anything, I want you to be happy. You are so loving and generous in your nature that you'll probably forgive her for what she's done— which is something I will never do, even should I live to be a thousand years old!' he declared extravagantly. 'So don't even begin to think that I arranged this for her out of anything but a desire to put your mind at rest.'

'Oh, I don't. I truly don't!' she assured him, smothering a giggle at his vehement protestations loving him all the more for his generosity towards a woman who had brought him nothing but trouble. 'But—' she shot upright so that she could see his beloved face '—I did have one nasty moment—even before Jilly told me those poisoned lies.'

'And that was?'

'When we arrived at where she's living. I felt as if you'd gone away from me. That you'd had it in mind that I'd set out to deceive you, pretend I was my twin and it had hit you that we were tarred with the same brush. Bad blood.'

'Never! Never think that—I absolutely forbid it!' He hooked a finger beneath her chin, his eyes scorching hers. 'For the first time in my life I was scared witless. Terrified that she would say or do something to come between us. I knew how you valued the bond you have with your twin, how you went against every natural inclination within you to try to protect her from me and what at that time you would have seen as my unfair accusations and threats of the courts. I was deeply afraid that somehow she would persuade you to stand beside her against me,' he confessed rawly. 'I can face any disaster with courage. But not that. I had not gone away from you, as you feared. I was simply afraid.'

'Cesare!' she managed shakily. That this wonderful man should love her so much and that what he had most feared had almost come about because it had taken her a good hour to work things out, think logically, shook her to the core. She coiled her arms around his neck, her voice a thread as she whispered, 'Kiss me.'

And he obliged with all the dedication and enthusiasm in the world.

Just over a year later Milly tucked baby Carlo into his muslin draped cradle while Maria, the comfortable nurse-maid Cesare had insisted they bring along to their villa in Amalfi, drew the nursery blinds.

Milly smiled besottedly down at her son. At three months old he was already showing signs of developing into a carbon copy of the devastatingly handsome, strong-willed father who adored him. She couldn't be happier! Wonderful was too tame a word to describe life with her sexy, masterful yet achingly tender husband.

Nonna had welcomed her into the family with genuine joy and had become even more sprightly since the birth of her first great-grandson and the only small cloud—a tiny one—in her life had dispersed when a couple of months ago Jilly had written out of the blue expressing her deep regrets for the lies she had told, confessing everything. That Cesare had never been interested in her and that sheer spite and malice that he had fallen for Milly had motivated her lies. She apolo-gized profusely for her behaviour and concluded with her own happy announcement. She had recently married on Teddy Myerburg, the third, a really great guy. Jilly was sorry not to have invited her but felt it would be too soon for her sister to forgive her, though she hoped that day might come.

Passing the letter to Cesare to read, she'd watched his jaw tighten, then left him to it and studied the photograph enclosed with the letter. Jilly, wearing a plain white sheath dress looked fantastic. And smug. Her groom was portly and balding and looked immensely proud. But not as proud as Cesare had looked when she'd walked down the aisle to him, wearing a fabulously expensive confection of white silk embroidered with seed pearls.

'Myerburg's a wealthy guy. I met him once in New York. A decent character. His first wife died. It took him a while to get over it, apparently. A bit old for her, but his money should keep her in line.' He passed the letter back. 'As for forgiving her, I imagine you already have. Maybe we'll invite them both over for the christening of our third child, when and if fortune blesses us and that happens.' He gave her that wicked grin that told her that it wouldn't be for the want of trying.

But if she never came face to face with her twin again that would be OK. Just knowing she was happy, had someone to care for her, was enough.

Bestowing one last loving look on her beautiful sleeping son, she left the nursery, meeting Cesare on his way there. Clad in wet swimming briefs, his hard male physique spangled with water droplets, he was enough to turn her knees to jelly.

'I've been in the pool,' he stated superfluously. 'I forgot the time. Have I missed bedtime?'

'You have. But he won't hold it against you.'

'Pity. It's the first time I missed out on tucking him in.' He reached for her, one hand at her tiny waist, the other busy with the tiny buttons on the front of her cool voile dress.

'To tell the truth, I was too busy fantasising about what I would do when you joined me to remember the time. Take this off and I'll turn fantasy into reality.'

'I've got a better idea. Much better. Her heartbeat accelerated. She took his hand and led him into their airy spacious bedroom. 'It's a good two hours before we eat.' When they were here they took their meals on the balcony overlooking the old town and the glorious panoramic view of the bay. 'Enough time, I think.'

'Just about,' he considered huskily, discarding her dress, his hands moving with practised ease to the fastening of her lacy bra. 'Do you know how much I adore you?'

'If it's half as much as I adore you,' she breathed, revelling in the sensation of wanton expectation as he slipped her matching briefs slowly down to her ankles, 'then I'll be satisfied.'

'Ah, but I'm insatiable! I'm always coming back for more, you should know that by now!' he groaned as he tumbled her on to the bed, shed his briefs and proceeded to show her exactly what he meant.